Jessi Ramsey, Pet-sitter

**Look for these and other books
in the Baby-sitters Club series:**

1 Kristy's Great Idea

2 Claudia and the
Phantom Phone Calls

3 The Truth About Stacey

4 Mary Anne Saves the Day

5 Dawn and the Impossible Three

6 Kristy's Big Day

7 Claudia and Mean Janine

8 Boy-Crazy Stacey

9 The Ghost at Dawn's House

#10 Logan Likes Mary Anne!

#11 Kristy and the Snobs

#12 Claudia and the New Girl

#13 Good-bye Stacey, Good-bye

#14 Hello, Mallory

#15 Little Miss Stoneybrook
. . . and Dawn

#16 Jessi's Secret Language

#17 Mary Anne's
Bad-Luck Mystery

#18 Stacey's Mistake

#19 Claudia and the Bad Joke

#20 Kristy and the
Walking Disaster

#21 Mallory and the
Trouble With Twins

#22 Jessi Ramsey, Pet-sitter

#23 Dawn on the Coast

Super Special:
Baby-sitters on Board!

Jessi Ramsey, Pet-sitter
Ann M. Martin

AN
APPLE
PAPERBACK

SCHOLASTIC INC.
New York Toronto London Auckland Sydney

Cover art by Hodges Soileau

ISBN 0-590-42006-2

12 11 10 9 8 7 6 5 4 3 2 1   9/8 0 1 2 3 4/9

Printed in the U.S.A.   28

First Scholastic printing, March 1989

This book is for my friends
Nicole, Anna, Rebecca,
Katie, and Alison

CHAPTER 1

"Meow, meow, meow. Purr, purr."

I leaned over the edge of my bed and peered down at the floor.

"Pet me," said a small voice.

It wasn't a talking animal. It was my sister, Becca, pretending she was a cat.

I patted the top of her head but said, "Becca, I really have to do my homework."

"Then how come you're lying on your bed?" asked Becca, getting to her feet.

"Because this is a comfortable way to work."

"You're supposed to sit at your desk."

This is true. My parents believe that homework magically gets done better if you're sitting up than if you're lying down.

I sighed. Then I changed the subject, which usually distracts Becca. "Why are you a cat tonight?" I asked her.

She shrugged. "I'm trying all the animals. It's fun to pretend."

The night before, Becca had been a dog, the night before that, a horse.

"Well, kitty, let me finish my work," I said.

"Meow," replied Becca, who dropped to her hands and knees and crawled into the hallway.

Becca is eight and has a big imagination. If she weren't so shy, she'd probably make a really terrific actress, but she has awful stage fright.

I do not have stage fright, which is lucky since I'm a ballet dancer and have to perform in front of audiences all the time.

I guess I should stop and introduce myself. I am Jessi Ramsey, and I'm eleven and in sixth grade. "Jessi" is short for "Jessica." (And "Becca" is short for "Rebecca," as if you couldn't have guessed.) Becca and I live with our parents and our baby brother, Squirt. Squirt's real name is John Philip Ramsey, Jr. When he was born, he was so tiny that the nurses in the hospital started calling him Squirt. Now his nickname seems sort of funny. Well, it always has been funny, but it seems especially funny since Squirt, who has just learned to walk, is now the size of most other babies his age.

Anyway, as I said before, I'm a ballet dancer. I've been taking dance classes for years. My ballet school is in Stamford, which isn't too far from Stoneybrook, Connecticut, where my family and I live. We haven't lived here long, though. We moved to Connecticut from New Jersey just a few months ago when my dad was offered a job he couldn't turn down.

Oh, something else about my family — we're black. Actually, that's much more important than I'm making it sound. You know what? It wasn't so important when we were living in Oakley, New Jersey. Our old neighborhood was mixed black and white, and so was my ballet school and my regular school. But believe it or not, we are one of the few black families in all of Stoneybrook. In fact, I'm the only black student in my whole grade. When we first moved here, some people weren't very nice to us. Some were even mean. But things have settled down and are getting better. Becca and I are making friends. Actually, I have a lot more friends than Becca does. There are two reasons for this: one, I'm not shy; two, I belong to the Baby-sitters Club. (More about that later.)

My mother is wonderful and so is my father. We're a very close family. Mama, Daddy, Becca, Squirt, and me. No pets. We've never had a pet, although Becca apparently wishes we had one. (Sometimes I do, too, for that matter.)

In case you're wondering what the Baby-sitters Club is, let me tell you about it. It's very important to me because that's where I found most of my friends. The club is really a business, a sitting business. It was started by Kristy Thomas, who's the president. There are six of us in the club. We sit for kids in our neighborhoods, and we get lots of jobs and have lots of fun.

My best friend in Stoneybrook is Mallory Pike. Mal and I have a lot of classes together at Stoneybrook Middle School. And Mal is the one who got me into the Baby-sitters Club. The girls needed another member and ended up taking both of us. We were just getting to be friends then — and now that we've been in the club together for awhile, we're best friends. (I have another best friend in Oakley — my cousin Keisha.)

Anyway, the people in the club are Mallory, Kristy, me, plus Claudia Kishi, Mary Anne Spier, and Dawn Schafer. Two people who are sort of part of the club but who don't come to our meetings are our associate members, Logan Bruno and Shannon Kilbourne. (I'll tell you more about them later.) It's funny that us six club members work so well together, because boy, are we different. We have different personalities, different tastes, different looks, and different kinds of families.

4

Kristy Thomas, our president, is . . . well, talk about not shy. Kristy is direct and outgoing. Sometimes she can be loud and bossy. But basically she's really nice. And she's always full of ideas. Kristy is thirteen and in eighth grade. (So are all the club members, except Mal and me.) She has this long brown hair and is pretty, but doesn't pay much attention to her looks. I mean, she never bothers with makeup, and she always wears jeans, a turtleneck, a sweater, and sneakers. Kristy's family is sort of interesting. Her parents are divorced, and for the longest time, Kristy lived with just her mom, her two older brothers, Sam and Charlie (they're in high school), and her little brother, David Michael, who's seven now. But when her mom met this millionaire, Watson Brewer, and got remarried, things sure changed for Kristy. For one thing, Watson moved Kristy's family into his mansion, which is on the other side of Stoneybrook. Kristy used to live next door to Mary Anne Spier and across the street from Claudia Kishi. Now she's in a new neighborhood. For another thing, Kristy acquired a little stepsister and stepbrother — Watson's children from his first marriage. Karen is six and Andrew is four. Although it took Kristy some time to adjust to her new life, she sure loves Karen and Andrew. They're among her favorite baby-sitting charges. Kristy's family has two pets — an adorable puppy named Shannon and a fat old cat named Boo-Boo.

The vice-president of the Baby-sitters Club is Claudia Kishi, and she is totally cool. I think she's the coolest person I know. (I mean, except for movie stars or people like that.) Claud is just awesome-looking. She's Japanese-American and has gorgeous, *long*, jet-black hair; dark, almond-shaped eyes; and a clear complexion. Really. She could be on TV as the "after" part of a pimple medicine commercial. Claud loves art, Nancy Drew mysteries, and junk food, and she hates school. She's smart, but she's a terrible student. (Unfortunately, her older sister, Janine, is a genius, which makes Claudia's grades look even worse.) Claudia also loves fashion, and you should see her clothes. They are amazing, always wild. Like, she'll wear a miniskirt, black tights, push-down socks, high-top sneakers, a shirt she's painted or decorated herself, and big earrings she's made. Her hair might be pulled into a ponytail and held in place with not one but six or seven puffy ponytail holders, a row of them cascading down her hair. I'm always fascinated by Claudia. Claud lives with Janine, her parents, and her grandmother, Mimi. The Kishis don't have any pets.

Mary Anne Spier is the club secretary. She lives across the street from Claudia. And, until Kristy's family moved, she lived next door to the Thomases. Mary Anne and Kristy are best friends, and have been pretty much for life. (Dawn is Mary Anne's other best friend.) I've always thought this was interesting, since Mary Anne and Kristy are not alike at all. Mary Anne is shy and quiet and, well, sort of romantic. (She's the only club member who has a steady boyfriend. And guess who he is — Logan Bruno, one of our associate members!) Mary Anne is also a good listener and a patient person. Her mom died years ago, so Mary Anne's father raised her, and for the longest time, he was strict with her. Boy, was he strict. I didn't know Mary Anne then, but I've heard that Mr. Spier made all these rules, and there was practically nothing she was allowed to do. Lately, Mr. Spier has relaxed, though. He won't let Mary Anne get her ears pierced, but at least she can go out with Logan sometimes, and she can choose her own clothes. Since she's been allowed to do that, she's started dressing *much* better — not as wildly as Claudia, but she cares about how she looks, unlike Kristy. Mary Anne's family is just her and her dad and her gray kitten, Tigger.

Dawn Schafer is the treasurer of the Baby-sitters Club. I like Dawn. She's neat. Dawn is neither loud like Kristy nor shy like Mary Anne. She's an individual. She'd never go along with something just because other people were doing it. And she always sticks up for what she believes in. Dawn is basically a California girl. She moved to Connecticut about a year ago, but she still longs for warm weather and she loves health food. She even *looks* like a California girl with her white-blonde hair and her sparkling blue eyes. Although you'd never know it, Dawn has been through some tough times lately. When she moved here, she came with her mother and her younger brother, Jeff — her parents had just gotten divorced. Mrs. Schafer wanted to live in Stoneybrook because she'd grown up here, but that put three thousand miles between Dawn's mother and Dawn's father. As if the divorce and the move weren't enough, Jeff finally decided he couldn't handle the East Coast and moved back to California, so now Dawn's family is cracked in two, like a broken plate. But Dawn seems to be handling things okay. Luckily, she has her best friend (Mary Anne), and she and her mother are *extremely* close. Just so you know, the Schafers live in a neat old farmhouse that has a secret passage (honest), and they don't have any pets.

Then there's Mallory. Mallory Pike and I are the club's two junior officers. All that means is that we're too young to baby-sit at night unless we're sitting for our own brothers and sisters. Speaking of brothers and sisters, Mal has *seven* of them. She comes from the biggest family I know. Apart from that, and apart from the fact that Mal is white and I'm black, we're probably more alike than any two other club members. We both love to read books, especially horse stories, we both enjoy writing (but Mal enjoys it more than I do), we both wear glasses (mine are only for reading), and we both think our parents treat us kind of like babies. However, there was a recent breakthrough in which we convinced our parents to let us get our ears pierced! After that, Mal was even allowed to have her hair cut decently, but I'm still working on that angle. Neither of us is sure what we want to be when we grow the rest of the way up. I *might* want to be a professional dancer and Mal *might* want to be an author or an author/illustrator, but we figure we have time to decide these things. Right now, we're just happy being eleven-year-old baby-sitters.

Oh, one other similarity between Mal and me. Neither of us has a pet. I don't know if Mal wants one — she's never mentioned it —

but I bet her brothers and sisters do. Just like Becca.

"Hiss, hiss."

Becca was in my doorway. She was lying on her stomach.

"Now what are you?" I asked.

"I'll give you a hint." Becca flicked her tongue out of her mouth.

"Ew, ew!" I cried. "You're a snake. Slither away from me!"

Giggling, Becca did as she was told.

I went back to my homework, but I couldn't concentrate. Not because of Becca, but because of next week. I was going to have next week off. Well, sort of. Ordinarily, my afternoons are busy. When school is out, I go either to a ballet class or to my steady sitting job. My steady job is for Matt and Haley Braddock, two really great kids. But next week, my ballet school would be closed and the Braddocks were going on a vacation — even though school was in session. So, except for school and meetings of the Baby-sitters Club, I would be free, free, free! What would I do with all those spare hours? I wondered. Easy. I could put in extra practice time, I could read. The possibilities were endless!

CHAPTER 2

"Hi! Hi, you guys! Sorry I'm late." I rushed breathlessly into the Wednesday meeting of the Baby-sitters Club.

"You're not late," said Kristy, our president. "You're just the last one here."

"As always," I added.

"Well, don't worry about it. But it *is* five-thirty and time to begin." Kristy sounded very businesslike.

Mallory patted the floor next to her, so I shoved aside some of Claudia's art materials and sat down. We always sit on the floor. And Dawn, Mary Anne, and Claudia always sit on Claudia's bed. Guess where Kristy sits—in a director's chair, wearing a visor, as if she were the queen or something.

Club meetings are held in Claudia Kishi's room. This is because she's the only one of us who has a phone in her bedroom, and her own personal, private phone number, which makes it easy for our clients to reach us.

Hmmm. . . . I think I better stop right here, before I get ahead of myself. I'll tell you how the club got started and how it works; then the meeting won't sound so confusing.

The club began with Kristy, as I said before. She got the idea for it over a year ago. That was when she and her mom and brothers were still living across the street from Claudia, and her mother was just starting to date Watson Brewer. Usually, when Mrs. Thomas wasn't going to be around, Kristy or Sam or Charlie would take care of David Michael. But one day when Mrs. Thomas announced that she was going to need a sitter, neither Kristy nor one of her older brothers was free. So Mrs. Thomas got on the phone and began calling around for another sitter. Kristy watched her mom make one call after another. And as she watched, that mind of hers was clicking away, thinking that Mrs. Thomas sure could save time if she could make one call and reach several sitters at once. And that was when Kristy got the idea for the Baby-sitters Club!

She talked to Mary Anne and Claudia, Claudia talked to Stacey McGill, a new friend of hers, and the four of them formed the club. (I'll tell you more about Stacey in a minute.)

The girls decided that they'd meet three times a week in Claudia's room (because of the phone). They'd advertise their club in the local paper and around the neighborhood, saying that four reliable sitters could be reached every Monday, Wednesday, and Friday afternoon from five-thirty until six.

Well, Kristy's great idea worked! Right away, the girls started getting jobs. People really liked them. In fact, the club was so successful that when Dawn moved to Stoneybrook and wanted to join, the girls needed her. And later, when Stacey McGill had to move back to New York City, they needed to replace her. (Stacey's move, by the way, was unfortunate, because in the short time the McGills lived in Stoneybrook, she and Claudia became best friends. Now they really miss each other.) Anyway, Mal and I joined the club to help fill the hole left by Stacey, and Shannon Kilbourne and Logan Bruno were made associate members. That means that they don't come to meetings, but if a job is offered that the rest of us can't take, we call one of them to see if they're interested. They're our backups. Believe it or not, we do have to call them every now and then.

Each person in the club holds a special

position or office. There are the associate members, Shannon and Logan, and there are the junior officers, Mal and me. The other positions are more important. (I'm not putting the rest of us down or anything. This is just the truth.)

As president, Kristy is responsible for running the meetings, getting good ideas, and, well, just being in charge, I guess. Considering that president is the most important office of all, Kristy doesn't do a lot of work. I mean, not compared to what the other girls do. But then, the club *was* her idea, so I think she deserves to be its president.

Claudia Kishi, our vice-president, doesn't really have a lot to do, either, but the rest of us invade her room three times a week and tie up her phone line. Plus, a lot of our clients forget when our meetings are held and call at other times with sitting jobs. Claud has to handle those calls. I think she deserves to be vice-president.

As secretary, Mary Anne Spier is probably the hardest-working officer. She's in charge of the record book, which is where we keep track of all club information: our clients' addresses and phone numbers, the money in the treasury (well, that's really Dawn's department), and most importantly, the appointment calendar.

Poor Mary Anne has to keep track of everybody's schedules (my ballet lessons, Claud's art classes, dentist appointments, etc.) *and* all of our baby-sitting jobs. When a call comes in, it's up to Mary Anne to see who's free. Mary Anne is neat and careful and hasn't made a scheduling mistake yet.

This is a miracle.

Dawn, our treasurer, is responsible for collecting dues from us club members every Monday, and for keeping enough money in the treasury so that we can pay Charlie, Kristy's oldest brother, to drive her to and from meetings, since she lives so far away now. The money is spent on other things, too, but we make sure we always have enough for Charlie. What else is the money spent on? Well, fun things, like food for club slumber parties. Also new materials for Kid-Kits.

I guess I haven't told you about Kid-Kits yet. They were one of Kristy's ideas. A Kid-Kit is a box (we each have one) that's been decorated and filled with our old toys and books and games, as well as a few new items such as crayons or sticker books. We bring them with us on some of our jobs and kids love them. The kits make us very popular baby-sitters! Anyway, every now and then we need treasury money to buy new crayons or something for the kits.

The last thing you need to know about is our club notebook. The notebook is like a diary. In it, each of us sitters has to write up every single job she goes on. Then we're supposed to read it once a week to find out what's been going on. Even though most of us don't like writing in the notebook, I have to admit that it's helpful. When I read it, I find out what's happening with the kids our club sits for, and also about baby-sitting problems and how they were handled. (The club notebook was Kristy's idea, of course.)

"Order, order!" Kristy was saying.

I had just settled myself on the floor.

"Wait a sec," Claudia interrupted. "Doesn't anyone want something to eat?"

Remember I said Claudia likes junk food? Well, that may have been an understatement. Claud *loves* junk food. She loves it so much that her parents have told her to stop eating so much of it. But Claud can't. She buys it anyway and then hides it in her room. At the moment, she's got a bag of potato chips under her bed, a package of licorice sticks in a drawer of her jewelry box, and a bag of M&M's in the pencil case in her notebook. She's very generous with it. She offers it around at the beginning of each meeting since we're starved by this time of day. And we eat up. (Well, sometimes Dawn doesn't since she's so into health food, but she *will* eat crackers or pretzels.)

"Ahem," said Kristy.

"Oh, come on. You know you'll eat something if I get it out," Claudia told her. Claudia usually stands up to Kristy.

"All right." Kristy sounded as cross as a bear, but this didn't prevent her from eating a handful of M&M's.

When the candy had been passed around, Kristy said, "*Now* are we ready?"

(She sure can be bossy.)

"Ready, Ms. Thomas," Claudia replied in a high, squeaky voice.

Everyone laughed, even Kristy.

We talked about some club business, and then the phone began to ring. The first call was from Mrs. Newton. She's the mother of Jamie and Lucy, two of the club's favorite sitting charges. Mary Anne scheduled Dawn for the job. Then the phone rang twice more. Jobs for Mal and Mary Anne. I was sort of relieved that so far, none of the jobs had been for next week. I was still looking forward to my week off.

Ring, ring.

Another call.

Claudia answered the phone. She listened for a moment and then began to look confused. "Mrs. Mancusi?" she said.

Kristy glanced up from the notebook, which she'd been reading. "Mrs. Mancusi?" she whispered to the rest of us. "She doesn't have any kids."

We listened to Claud's end of the conversation, but all she would say were things like, "Mm-hmm," and "Oh, I see," and "Yes, that's too bad." Then, after a long pause, she said, "Well, this is sort of unusual, but let me talk to the other girls and see what they say. Someone will call you back in about five minutes. . . . Yes. . . . Okay. . . . Okay, 'bye."

Claudia hung up the phone and looked up from some notes she'd been making. She found the rest of us staring at her.

"Well?" said Kristy.

"Well, the Mancusis need a pet-sitter," Claudia began.

"A *pet*-sitter?" Kristy practically jumped down Claud's throat.

"Yeah, let me explain," Claud rushed on. "They're going on vacation next week. They've had this really nice vacation planned for months now. And you know all those animals they have?"

18

"Their house is a zoo," Mary Anne spoke up.

"I know," Claud replied. "All I could hear in the background was barking and squawking and chirping."

"What's the point?" asked Kristy rudely.

"Sheesh," said Claud. "Give me a minute. The *point* is that the Mancusis had a pet-sitter all lined up and he just called and canceled."

"That is *so* irresponsible," commented Mallory.

"I know," agreed Claud. "Now the Mancusis can't take their vacation, not unless they find a pet-sitter."

"Oh, but Claudia," wailed Kristy, "how could you even *think* about another pet-sitting job?"

"Another one?" I asked.

"Yeah," said Kristy. "The very first job I got when we started the club — my first job offer at our first official meeting — was for two Saint Bernard dogs, and it was a disaster."

I couldn't help giggling. "It was?" I said. "What happened?"

"Oh, you name it. The dogs, Pinky and Buffy, were sweet, but they were big and gallumphing and they liked making mischief. What an afternoon that was! Anyway, I swore we would never pet-sit again."

"But Kristy," protested Claudia, "if the Mancusis can't find a pet-sitter, they'll have to cancel their dream vacation."

Kristy sighed. "All right. Suppose one of us was crazy enough to *want* to pet-sit — don't the Mancusis need someone every day?"

"Yes, for a few hours every day next week, plus the weekend before and the weekend after. They're leaving this Saturday and returning Sunday, a week later."

"Well, that kills it," said Kristy. "I don't want any of my sitters tied up for a week."

At that, I heard Dawn mutter something that sounded like . . . well, it didn't sound nice. And I saw her poke Mary Anne, who mouthed "bossy" to her. Then Mal whispered to me, "Who does Kristy think she is? The queen?"

All of which gave me the courage to say (nervously), "Um, you know how the Braddocks are going away?"

"Yes?" replied the other club members, turning toward me.

"Well . . . well, um, my ballet school is closed next week, too. Remember? So I'm available. For the whole week. I could take care of the Mancusis' pets. I mean, if they want me to." (So much for my week of freedom.)

"Perfect!" exclaimed Claud. "I'll call them right now."

"Not so fast!" interrupted Kristy. "I haven't given my permission yet."

"Your per*miss*ion?" cried the rest of us.

Kristy must have realized she'd gone too far then. Her face turned bright red.

"Listen, just because *you* had a bad pet-sitting experience — " Dawn began.

"I know, I know. I'm sorry." Kristy turned toward me. "Go ahead," she said. "You may take the job."

"Thank you."

Claud called Mrs. Mancusi back, as promised. As you can probably imagine, Mrs. Mancusi was delighted to have a sitter. She asked to speak to me. After thanking me several times, she said, "When could you come by? My husband and I will have to show you how to care for the animals. There are quite a lot of them, you know."

After some discussion, we decided on Friday evening, right after supper. It was the only time the Mancusis and I were all free. Since the Mancusis live near my house, I knew that would be okay with my parents.

I hung up the phone. "Gosh, the Mancusis sure are going to pay me well."

"They better," Kristy replied. "I don't think Claud told you exactly how many pets they have. There are three dogs, five cats, some birds and hamsters, two guinea pigs, a snake, lots of fish, and a bunch of rabbits and turtles."

I gulped. What had I gotten myself into?

CHAPTER 3

As soon as I saw Mr. and Mrs. Mancusi, I realized I knew them — and they knew me. They're always out walking their dogs, and I'm often out walking Squirt in his stroller, or baby-sitting for some little kids. The Mancusis and I wave and smile at each other. Until I met them, I just didn't know their names, or that beside their dogs they owned a small zoo.

This is what I heard when I rang their doorbell: *Yip-yip, meow, mew, chirp, cheep, squawk, squeak, woof-woof-woof.*

By the way, I am a pretty good speller and every now and then my teacher gives me a list of really hard words to learn to spell and use in sentences. On the last list was the word *cacophony*. It means a jolting, nonharmonious mixture of sounds. Well, those animal voices at the Mancusis' were not jolting, but they sure were nonharmonious and they sure were a mixture.

The door opened. There was Mrs. Mancusi's pleasant face. "Oh! It's *you!*" she exclaimed, just as I said, "Oh! The dogwalker!"

"Come on in." Smiling, Mrs. Mancusi held the door open for me.

I stepped inside and the cacophony grew louder.

"SHH! SHH!" said Mrs. Mancusi urgently. "Sit. . . . Sit, Cheryl."

A Great Dane sat down obediently. Soon the barking stopped. Then the birds quieted down.

Mrs. Mancusi smiled at me. "So you're Jessi," she said. "I've seen you around a lot lately."

"We moved here a few months ago," I told her, not mentioning that, in general, the neighbors hadn't been too . . . talkative.

Mrs. Mancusi nodded. "Is that your brother I see you with sometimes?" she asked. (A bird swooped into the room and landed on her shoulder while a white kitten tottered to her ankles and began twining himself around them.)

"Yes," I answered. "That's Squirt. Well, his real name is John Philip Ramsey, Junior. I have a sister, too. Becca. She's eight. But," I added, "we don't have any pets."

Mrs. Mancusi looked fondly at her animals. "I guess that makes us even," she said. "My husband and I don't have any children, but we have plenty of pets. Well, I should start — "

At that moment, Mr. Mancusi strode into the front hall. After more introductions, his wife said, "I was just about to have Jessi meet the animals."

Mr. Mancusi nodded. "Let's start with the dogs. I guess you've already seen Cheryl," he said, patting the Great Dane.

"Right," I replied. I pulled a pad of paper and a pencil out of my purse so I could take notes.

But Mr. Mancusi stopped me. "Don't bother," he said. "Everything is written down. We'll show you where in a minute. Just give the animals a chance to get to know you. In fact," he went on, "why don't you talk to each one? That would help them to feel more secure with you."

"Talk to them?" I repeated.

"Sure. Say anything you want. Let them hear the sound of your voice."

I felt like a real jerk, but I patted the top of Cheryl's head (which is softer than it looks) and said, "Hi, Cheryl. I'm Jessi. I'm going to walk you and take care of you next week."

Cheryl look at me with her huge eyes — and yawned.

We all laughed. "I guess I'm not very impressive," I said.

On the floor in the living room lay an apricot-colored poodle.

"That's Pooh Bear," said Mrs. Mancusi. "Believe it or not, she's harder to walk than Cheryl. Cheryl is big but obedient. Pooh Bear is small but devilish."

I knelt down and patted Pooh Bear's curly fur. "Nice girl," I said. (Pooh Bear stared at me.) "Nice girl . . . Um, I'm Jessi. We're going to take walks next week." Then I added in a whisper, "I hope you'll behave."

The Mancusis' third dog is a golden retriever named Jacques. Jacques was napping in the kitchen. He tiredly stuck his paw in my lap when I sat down next to him, but he barely opened his eyes.

"Now Jacques," began Mr. Mancusi, "is only a year old. Still pretty much a puppy. He tries hard to behave, but if Pooh Bear acts up, he can't help following her lead."

"Right," I said. I tried to think of something creative to say to Jacques, but finally just told him I was looking forward to walking him.

"All right. Cats next," said Mrs. Mancusi, picking up the kitten. "This little fluffball is Powder. He's just two and a half months old. But don't worry. He knows how to take care of himself. Also, his mother is here."

"Hi, Powder," I said, putting my face up to his soft fur.

Then Mrs. Mancusi set Powder on the ground and we went on a cat-hunt, in search of the other four. Here's who we found: Crosby, an orange tiger cat who can fetch like a dog; Ling-Ling, a Siamese cat with a *very* loud voice; Tom, a patchy gray cat with a wicked temper; and Rosie, Powder's mother.

Next we went into the Mancusis' den, where there were several large bird cages holding parakeets, cockatoos, and macaws.

"Awk?" said one bird as we entered the room. "Where's the beef? Where's the beef? Where's the beef?"

Mr. Mancusi laughed. "That's Frank," he said. "He used to watch a lot of TV. I mean, before we got him." I must have looked astonished, because he went on, "It's natural for some birds to imitate what they hear. Frank can say other things, too, can't you, Frank?"

Frank blinked his eyes but remained silent.

"See, he isn't really trained," added Mr. Mancusi. "He only talks when he feels like it."

Mrs. Mancusi removed the bird that had landed on her shoulder earlier and placed him in one of the cages. "Often, we leave the cages open," she told me, "and let the birds fly around the house. I'd suggest it for next week, but most people don't feel comfortable trying to get the birds back in the cages, so maybe that's not such a good idea."

It certainly didn't sound like a good one to me.

I started to leave the den, but Mr. Mancusi was looking at me, so I peered into the bird cages and spoke to Frank and his friends.

In the kitchen were a cage full of hamsters and a much bigger cage, almost a pen, that contained two guinea pigs. I looked in at the hamsters first.

"They're nocturnal," said Mrs. Mancusi. "They're up all night and asleep all day. You should see them in the daytime. They sleep in a big pile in the middle of the cage."

I smiled. Then I looked at the guinea pigs. They were pretty interesting, too. They were big, bigger than the hamsters, and they were sniffing around their cage. Every so often one of them would let out a whistle.

"The guinea pigs are Lucy and Ricky. You know, from the *I Love Lucy* show," said Mr. Mancusi. "They shouldn't be any trouble, and they *love* to be taken out of their cage for exercise."

"Okay," I said, thinking that Lucy and Ricky looked like fun.

We left the kitchen and walked toward a sun porch. The job, I decided, was going to be big but manageable. I could handle it.

Then I met the reptiles.

The aquarium full of turtles wasn't *too* bad. I don't love turtles, but I don't mind them.

What was bad was Barney.

Barney is a snake. He's very small and he isn't poisonous, but he's still a snake. A wriggling, scaly, tongue-flicking snake.

Thank goodness the Mancusis didn't ask me to touch Barney or take him out of his cage. All they said was I'd have to feed him. Well, I could do that. Even if I did have to feed him the insects and earthworms that the Mancusis had a supply of. I'd just try to wear oven mitts. Or maybe I could stand ten feet away from his cage and throw the worms in.

"Nice Barney. Good Barney," I whispered when the Mancusis stopped and waited for me to talk to him. "You don't hurt me — and I'll stay away from you."

Next the Mancusis showed me their fish (about a million of them), and their rabbits (Fluffer-Nut, Cindy, Toto, and Robert). And after *that*, they took me back to the kitchen, where they had posted lists of instructions for caring for each type of animal, plus everything I'd need to feed and exercise them — food dishes, chow (several kinds), leashes, etc. I would be going to their house twice a day. Early in the morning to walk the dogs and feed the dogs and cats, and after school to walk the dogs again and to feed all the animals.

When I said good-night to the Mancusis I felt slightly overwhelmed but confident. The job was a big one, but I'd met the animals, and I'd seen the lists of instructions. They were very clear. If the animals would just behave, everything would be fine . . . probably.

Saturday was my test. The Mancusis left late in the morning. By the middle of the afternoon, Cheryl, Pooh Bear, and Jacques would be ready for a walk. After that, the entire zoo would need feeding. So at three o'clock I headed for the Mancusis' with the key to their front door. I let myself in (the cacophony began immediately), managed to put leashes on the dogs, and took them for a nice, long walk. The walk went fine except for when Pooh Bear spotted a squirrel. For just a moment, the dogs were taking *me* on a walk instead of the other way around. But the squirrel disappeared, the dogs calmed down, and we returned to the Mancusis' safely.

When the dog's leashes had been hung up, I played with the cats and the guinea pigs. I let the rabbits out for awhile. Then it was feeding time. Dog chow in the dog dishes, cat chow in the cat dishes, fish food in the tank, rabbit food in the hutch, guinea pig food in the guinea pig cage, bird food in the bird cages, turtle food in the aquarium, hamster food in the hamster cage, and finally it was time for . . . Barney.

I looked in his cage. There he was, sort of twined around a rock. He wasn't moving, but his eyes were open. I think he was looking at me. I found a spatula in the kitchen, used it to slide the lid of Barney's cage back, and then, quick as a wink, I dropped his food inside and shoved the lid closed.

Barney never moved.

Well, that was easy, I thought as I made a final check on all the animals. A lot of them were eating. But the hamsters were sound asleep. They were all sleeping in a pile, just like Mrs. Mancusi had said they would do, except for one very fat hamster. He lay curled in a corner by himself. What was wrong? Was he some sort of outcast? I decided not to worry, since the Mancusis hadn't said anything about him.

I found my house key and got ready to go. My first afternoon as a pet-sitter had been a success, I decided.

CHAPTER 4

Sundae

Oh, my lord waht a day. I babbysat for Jamie newton and he invinted Nina marshal over to play. That was fine but I thoght it would be fun for the kids to see all the amials over at the ~~the~~ ~~thar~~ makusees or however you spell it. So I took them over but Jamie was afriad of the ginny pigs so we took the kids and the dogs on a walk but we ran into Chewey and you now waht that means -- trouble.

Well, it was trouble, as Claudia said, but it wasn't too bad. I mean, I'm sure we've all been in worse trouble.

Anyway, on Sunday afternoon when I was about to head back to the Mancusis', Claudia was baby-sitting for Jamie Newton. Jamie is four, and one of the club's favorite clients. Kristy, Mary Anne, and Claudia were sitting for him long before there even *was* a Baby-sitters Club. Now Jamie has an eight-month-old sister, Lucy, but Claud was only in charge of Jamie that day. His parents were going visiting, and they were taking Lucy with them.

When Claudia arrived at the Newtons', she found an overexcited Jamie. He was bouncing around, singing songs, making noises, and annoying everybody — which is not like Jamie.

"I don't know where he got all this energy," said Mrs. Newton tiredly. "I hope you don't mind, but I told him he could invite Nina Marshall to play. Maybe they'll run off some of Jamie's energy. Anyway, Nina is on her way over."

"Oh, that's fine," said Claud, who has sat for Nina and her little sister Eleanor many times.

The Newtons left then, and Claudia took Jamie outside to wait for Nina.

"Miss Mary Mack, Mack, Mack," sang Jamie, jumping along the front walk in time to his song, "all dressed in black, black, black, with silver buttons, buttons, buttons, all down her back, back, back. She jumped so high, high, high," (Jamie's jumping became even bouncier at that part) "she touched the sky, sky, sky, and didn't come back, back, back, till the Fourth of July, ly, ly!"

Lord, thought Claudia, I have hardly ever seen Jamie so wound up.

Unfortunately, Jamie didn't calm down much when Nina arrived. Claudia suggested a game of catch — and in record time, an argument broke out.

"If you miss the ball, you have to give up your turn," announced Jamie.

"Do not!" cried Nina indignantly.

"Do too!"

"Do not!"

"Whoa!" said Claudia, taking the ball from Jamie. "I think that's enough catch. Let's find something else to do today."

"Miss Mary Mack, Mack, Mack — " began Jamie.

Claudia didn't want to listen to the song

again. She racked her brain for some kind of diversion — and had an idea. "Hey, you guys," she said excitedly, "how would you like to go to a place where you can see lots of animals?"

"The *zoo?*" exclaimed Nina.

"Almost," Claud replied. "*Do* you want to see some animals?"

"Yes!" cried Jamie and Nina.

"Okay," said Claud. "Nina, I'm just going to call your parents and tell them where we're going. Then we can be on our way."

Fifteen minutes later the Mancusis' doorbell was ringing. I had arrived to do the afternoon feeding and walking. As you can imagine, I was surprised. Who would be ringing their bell? Somebody who didn't know they were on vacation, I decided.

I peeked out the front windows before I went ahead and opened the door. And standing on the stoop were Claud, Jamie Newton, and Nina Marshall! I let them in right away.

"Hi, you guys!" I exclaimed.

"Hi," replied Claud. "I hope we're not bothering you."

"Nope. I just got here. I'm getting ready to walk the dogs."

"Oh," said Claudia. "Well, if it isn't too much trouble, could Jamie and Nina look at the animals? We're sort of on a field trip."

I giggled. "Sure. I'll show you around."

But I didn't have to do much showing at first. Pooh Bear was lolling on the floor in the front hall, and then Rosie wandered in, followed by Powder, who was batting his mother's tail.

Jamie and Nina began patting Pooh Bear and Rosie and trying to cuddle Powder. When the animals' patience wore out, I took Jamie and Nina by the hand and walked them to the bird cages. Frank very obligingly called out, "Where's the beef? Where's the beef?" and then, "Two, two, two mints in one!"

"Gosh," said Jamie, "I know a song you'd like, Frank." He sang Miss Mary Mack to him. "See?" he went on. "Miss Mary Mack, Mack, Mack. It's kind of like 'Two, two, two mints in one!' "

Next I showed the kids the rabbits and then the guinea pigs.

"We can take the guinea pigs out — " I started to say.

But Jamie let loose a shriek. "NO! NO! Don't take them out!"

"Hey," said Claud, wrapping Jamie in her arms, "don't worry. We won't take them out. What's wrong?"

"They're beasties!" Jamie cried. "They come from outer space. I saw them on TV."

"Oh Jamie," Claud said gently. "They aren't beasties. There's no such — "

"*Beast*ies?" exclaimed Nina.

"Yes," said Jamie. "They're mean and awful. They bite people and then they take over the world."

"WAHHH!" wailed Nina. "I want to go home!"

I nudged Claudia. "Listen," I said, "I have to walk the dogs now anyway. Why don't you and Jamie and Nina come with me?"

"Good idea," agreed Claudia.

Jamie and Nina calmed down as they watched me put the leashes on Pooh Bear, Jacques, and Cheryl.

"Can Nina and I walk a dog?" asked Jamie.

"I'd really like to let you," I told him, "But the dogs are my responsibility. The Mancusis think *I'm* caring for them, so I better walk them. I'll bet you've never seen one person walk three dogs at the same time."

"No," agreed Jamie, as I locked the front door behind us. He and Nina watched, wide-eyed, as I took the leashes in my right hand and the dogs practically pulled me to the sidewalk.

Claud laughed, I laughed, and Jamie and Nina shrieked with delight.

The beasties were forgotten.

"I'll walk you back to your neighborhood," I told Claudia.

"You mean *Cheryl* will walk us back to our neighborhood," said Claud with a grin.

Cheryl was trying hard to be obedient, but she's so big that even when she walked, Jamie and Nina had to run to keep up with her.

"Actually," I told Claudia, "Pooh Bear is the problem. She's the feisty one. And when she gets feisty, Jacques gets feisty."

"Well, so far so good," Claud replied.

And everything was still okay by the time we reached Claudia's house. Just a few more houses and Jamie would be home again.

That was when Chewbacca showed up.

Who is Chewbacca? He's the Perkinses' black Labrador retriever. The Perkinses are the family who moved into Kristy Thomas' old house, across the street from Claudia. We sit for them a lot, since they have three kids — Myriah, Gabbie, and Laura. But guess what? It's harder to take care of Chewy by himself than to take care of all three girls together. Chewy isn't mean; don't get me wrong. He's just mischievous. Like Cheryl, he's big and lovable, but he gets into things. You can almost hear him thinking, Let's see. *Now* what can I do? Chewy finds things, hides things, chases things. And when you walk him, you never know what might catch his eye — a falling leaf, a butterfly — and cause him to go on a doggie rampage.

"Uh-oh, Chewy's loose!" said Claudia.

"Go home, Chewy! Go on home!" I coaxed him. I pointed to the Perkinses' house (as if Chewy would know what that meant).

Jamie added, "Shoo! Shoo!"

Chewy grinned at us and then pranced right up to the Mancusis' dogs. He just made himself part of the bunch, even though he wasn't on a leash.

"Well, now what?" I said as we walked along. Cheryl and Jacques and Pooh Bear didn't seem the least bit upset — but what would I do with Chewy when we got back to the Mancusis'? . . . And what would happen if Chewy saw something that set him off?

"Turn around," suggested Claudia. "Let's walk Chewy back to his house."

Jamie, Nina, Claudia, Pooh Bear, Jacques, Cheryl, and I turned around and headed for the Perkinses'. But Chewy didn't come with us. He sat on the sidewalk and waited for us to come back to him.

"He is just too smart," remarked Jamie.

I rang the Perkinses' bell, hoping someone would go get Chewy, but nobody answered.

"I guess he'll just have to walk with us," I finally said.

We rejoined Chewy and set off. Chewy bunched up with the dogs again as if he'd been walking with them all his life.

"Oh, no! There's a squirrel!" Claudia cried softly. "Now what?"

Chewy looked at the squirrel. The squirrel looked at Chewy.

Pooh Bear looked at the squirrel. The squirrel looked at Pooh Bear. Then it ran up a tree.

Nothing.

The rest of the walk was like that. A leaf drifted to the ground in front of the dogs. "Uh-oh," said Nina. But nothing happened. A chipmunk darted across the sidewalk. We all held our breaths, sure that Chewy or Pooh Bear or maybe Jacques was going to go off his (or her) rocker. But the dogs were incredibly well-behaved. It was as if they were trying to drive us crazy with their good behavior.

We circled around Claudia's neighborhood and finally reached the Perkinses' again. This time they were home and glad to see Chewy. We left him there, and then Claud took Jamie and Nina home, and I returned to the Mancusis' with the dogs. I played with the cats and guinea pigs and rabbits, and I fed the animals. In the hamster cage, the fat one was still curled in a separate corner. I wondered if I should be worried about him. When I stroked him with my finger, he didn't even wake up. I decided to keep my eye on him.

CHAPTER 5

On Monday afternoon I raced to the Mancusis', gave the dogs a whirlwind walk, played with the animals, fed them, and then raced to Claudia's for a club meeting. I just made it.

When I reached Claudia's room, Kristy was already in the director's chair, visor in place, the club notebook in her lap. But it was only 5:28. Two more minutes until the meeting would officially begin. Dawn hadn't arrived yet. (For once I wasn't the last to arrive!) Claudia was frantically trying to read the last two pages of *The Clue of the Velvet Mask*, a Nancy Drew mystery. Mary Anne was examining her hair for split ends, and Mallory was blowing a gigantic bubble with strawberry gum.

I joined Mal on the floor.

"Hi," I said.

Mal just waved, since she was concentrating on her bubble.

"Hi, Jessi," said Claudia and Mary Anne.

But Kristy was engrossed in the notebook and didn't say anything. When Dawn came in, she snapped to attention, though.

"Order, please!" she called. "Come to order."

Reluctantly, Claudia put her book down. "Just one *paragraph* to go," she said.

"Well, nothing ever happens in the last paragraph," remarked Mary Anne. "The author just tells you which mystery Nancy's going to solve next."

"That's true."

"ORDER!" shouted Kristy.

Boy, was I glad I was already *in* order.

"Sheesh," said Claud.

Kristy ignored her. "Ahem," she said. "Dawn, how's the treasury?"

"It'll be great after I collect dues," replied Dawn.

Groan, groan, groan. Every Monday Dawn collects dues, and every Monday we groan about having to give her money. It's not as if it's any big surprise. But the same thing —

"Please pay attention!" barked Kristy.

My head snapped up. What was this? School?

I glanced at Mallory who mouthed, "Bosslady" to me and nodded toward Kristy. Then I had to try not to laugh.

"All right," Kristy went on, "has everyone been reading the notebook?"

"Yes," we chorused. We *always* keep up with it.

"Okay," said Kristy. "If you're really reading it — "

"We are!" Claud exploded. "Sheesh, Kristy, what's with you lately? You're bossier than ever."

For a moment, Kristy softened. "Sorry," she said. "It's just that Charlie suddenly thinks he's the big shot of the world. Next year he'll be in college, you know. So he bosses Sam and David Michael and me around nonstop." Kristy paused. Then her face hardened into her "I am the president" look.

"But," she went on, "I *am* the president, which gives me the right to boss you club members around."

"Excuse me," said Claudia in an odd voice, and I wondered what was coming, "but as president just what else *do* you do — besides get ideas, which any of us could do."

"Oh, yeah?" said Kristy.

"Yeah."

"Well, what brilliant ideas have you had?"

"I believe," Mary Anne spoke up, "that Claudia was the one who designed the alphabet blocks that say The Baby-sitters Club. That's our logo and we use it on every flier we give out."

"Thank you, Mary Anne," said Claudia. "And I believe that Mary Anne figured out who sent her the bad-luck charm, which was the first step in solving that mystery a while ago."

"And Mallory — " I began.

"Okay, okay, okay," said Kristy.

But the other girls weren't finished.

"I," said Dawn, "would like to know, Kristy, just what it is — "

Ring, ring.

We were so engrossed in what Dawn was saying that we didn't all dive for the phone as usual.

Ring, ring.

Finally Mary Anne answered it. She arranged a job for Mallory. Then the phone rang two more times. When *those* jobs had been set up, we looked expectantly at Dawn. (Well, Kristy didn't. She was glaring at us — all of us.)

Dawn picked up right where she'd left off. " — just what it is you do besides boss us around and get great ideas."

"I run the meetings."

"Big deal," said Claudia.

"Well, what do *you* do, Ms. Vice-President?" asked Kristy hotly.

"Besides donating my room and my phone to you three times a week," Claudia replied, "I have to take all those calls that come in when we're not meeting. And there are quite a few of them. You know that."

"And," spoke up Dawn, "*I* have to keep track of the money, collect dues every week — which isn't always easy — and be in charge of remembering to pay your brother, and of buying things for the Kid-Kits."

"*I*," said Mary Anne, "probably have the most complicated job of anybody." (No one disagreed with her.) "I have to schedule *every single* job any of us goes on. I have to keep track of our schedules, of our clients, their addresses, and how many kids are in their families. It is a huge job."

"And we do these jobs *in addition* to getting ideas," pointed out Dawn.

There was a moment of silence. Then Mary Anne said, "Okay. We have a problem. But I've got an idea. I suggest — "

"We do *not* have a problem," Kristy interrupted her. "Trust me, we don't. All you guys need to do is calm down and you'll see that things are actually in control." Kristy paused. When none of us said anything, she went on, "Okay, now I have a really important idea.

Forget this other stuff. To make sure that each of you is reading the notebook once a week, I'm going to draw up a checklist. Every Monday, in order to show me you've been keeping up with the notebook, you'll initial a box on the chart."

"*What?!*" exclaimed Claudia.

Dawn and Mary Anne gasped.

Mallory and I glanced at each other. We hadn't been saying much. We didn't want to get involved in a club fight. Since we're the newest and youngest members, we try to stay out of arguments. It's hard to know whose side to be on. We don't want to step on any toes. And the easiest way to do that is to keep our mouths shut.

But the other girls *wanted* us to take sides.

"Jessi, what do you think?" asked Claudia. "Mallory?"

I hesitated. "About the chart?" I finally said.

"Yes, about the chart."

"Well, um, I — I mean . . ." I looked at Mal.

"See," Mal began, "um, it — I . . ."

Claudia was thoroughly annoyed. "Forget it," she snapped.

"Kristy, there is absolutely no reason to make a checklist for us," said Dawn. "There's not even any reason to *ask* us if we've been reading the notebook. We always keep up with it. Each one of us. Don't we say yes every time you ask us about it?"

The argument was interrupted by several more job calls. But as soon as Mary Anne had made the arrangements, the club members went right back to their discussion.

"There's no need for the checklist," Dawn said again.

"Don't you trust us?" Mary Anne wanted to know.

Kristy sighed. "Of course I trust you. The checklist will just, well, prove to me that I can trust you. Plus, I won't have to ask you about reading the notebook anymore."

"But can't you *just trust* us?" said Mary Anne.

Kristy opened her mouth to answer the question, but Dawn spoke up instead.

"You know," she said, changing the subject, "personally, I am tired of having to collect dues on Mondays. Everyone groans and complains and makes me feel about *this* big." Dawn held her fingers a couple of inches apart.

"We don't mean to complain — " I started to tell Dawn.

But Claudia cut in with, "Well, *I'm* pretty tired of getting those job calls all the time. You know, some people don't even try to remember when our meetings are. Mrs. Barrett hardly ever calls during meetings. She calls at nine o'clock on a Sunday night, or on a Tuesday afternoon, or — worst of all — at eight-thirty on a Saturday morning."

"And I," said Mary Anne, "am especially tired of scheduling. I'm tired of keeping track of dentist appointments and ballet lessons — "

"Sorry," I apologized again. (I am really wonderful at apologizing.)

"Oh, it's not your fault, Jessi. Everyone has things that need scheduling. In fact, that's the problem. I'm up to my ears in lessons and classes and dental visits. I've been doing this job for over a year now, and I'm just tired of it. That's all there is to it."

"What are you guys saying?" Kristy asked her friends.

"That I don't like scheduling," Mary Anne replied.

"And I don't like collecting dues," said Dawn.

"And I don't like all the phone calls," added Claudia.

I looked at Mal. Why didn't Kristy speak up? What did she not like about being president? Finally it occurred to me — nothing. There was nothing she didn't like be- cause . . . because her job was pretty easy and fun. Conducting meetings, being in charge, getting ideas. Kristy sure had the easy job. (Mal and I did, too, but we had been *made* junior officers with hardly any club responsibilities. We hadn't had a say in the matter.)

I think we were all relieved when the meeting broke up. Well, I know Mal and I were, but it was hard to tell about the others. They left the meeting absolutely silently. Not a word was spoken.

Mal and I stood around on the sidewalk in front of the Kishis' until the other girls left. As soon as Mary Anne had disappeared into her house across the street, I said, "Whoa. Some meeting. What do you think, Mal?"

"I think," she replied, "that this is not a good sign. I also think that you and I might be asked to take sides soon."

"Probably," I agreed, "but it's going to be very important that we stay neutral. No taking sides at all."

CHAPTER 6

Tuesday

Oh, wow. I don't have words to describe what happened today. I could write down awful, disgusting, gross, shivery, blechh, but even those words don't say it all. I better just explain what happened. See, I was baby-sitting for Myriah and Gabbie Perkins, and I decided to take them over to the Mancusis' to visit the animals. I knew Claudia had done that with Jamie and Nina, and I thought it was a good idea. (How did I know Claudia had done that? Because I read the notebook, Kristy, that's how.) So I walked the girls over to the Mancusis'....

Mary Anne just loves sitting for the Perkinses. Remember them? They're the owners of Chewy; they're the family who moved into Kristy's house after the Thomases left it for Watson's mansion. The three Perkins girls are Myriah, who's five and a half, Gabbie Ann, who's two and a half, and Laura, the baby. Laura is so little that we usually don't take care of her, just Myriah and Gabbie. Right now, Laura pretty much goes wherever her mother goes.

Myriah and Gabbie are fun and us sitters like them a lot. The girls enjoy adventures and trying new things, which was why Mary Anne thought they'd like the trip to the Mancusis'. And they did like it. The awful-disgusting-gross-shivery-blechh thing had nothing to do with the girls. In fact, Mary Anne was the one who caused it. Myriah helped to solve it.

I better back up a little here. Okay, at about four o'clock on Tuesday afternoon I returned to the Mancusis' after walking the dogs, and found the phone ringing.

"Hello, Mancusi residence," I said breathlessly as I picked up the phone.

"Hi, Jessi, it's Mary Anne."

Mary Anne was calling to find out if she

could bring Myriah and Gabbie over. I told her yes, of course, and about twenty minutes later they showed up.

"Oh, boy! Aminals!" cried Gabbie. Her blonde hair was fixed in two ponytails that bobbed up and down as she made a dash for the Mancusis' kitchen.

"All kinds!" added Myriah. Myriah's hair was pulled back into one long ponytail that reached halfway down her back. She followed her sister.

The girls began exploring the house. The cats and dogs weren't too interesting to them since they've got one of each at their house — Chewy, and their cat, R.C. But the other animals fascinated them.

I showed them Barney. I showed them Lucy and Ricky. I explained everything I could think of to them. We moved on.

"These are — "

"Easter bunnies!" supplied Gabbie, as we looked in at Fluffer-Nut, Robert, Toto, and Cindy.

"You can hold them," I said. "The rabbits like to have a chance to get out of their hutch."

So Myriah held Toto, and Gabbie held Fluffer-Nut. For a few minutes, the girls had a giggle-fest. I looked around for Mary Anne.

When I didn't see her, I was relieved instead of worried. I didn't want to talk about Kristy or our club problems with her.

Soon the girls grew tired of the rabbits, so we put them back.

"Now these," I told Gabbie and Myriah, "are hamsters. Since they're sleeping, we won't disturb them. But see how fat that hamster's face is?" I pointed to one on top of the pile of hamsters. It was not the fat hamster. He was still off by himself in that corner of the cage. He seemed to have made a sort of nest. No, I pointed to one of the other hamsters.

"He looks like he has the mumps!" said Myriah.

"He does, doesn't he? But his fat cheeks are really — "

"AUGHHH!"

The scream came from the direction of the sun porch.

"Mary Anne?" I called.

"AUGHHH!" was her reply.

I put the lid back on the hamster cage, took Myriah and Gabbie by their hands, and ran with them to the sun porch.

A truly horrible sight met our eyes. We saw Barney's cage and the lid to Barney's cage — but no Barney.

"Mary Anne, what on earth happened?" I cried.

"Barney's loose!" was her response. "The *snake* is *loose!*"

Mary Anne and I got the same idea at the same time. We jumped up on one of the big porch chairs, the way people do when they've just seen a mouse.

Myriah and Gabbie looked at us as if we were crazy.

"What are you *do*ing?" exclaimed Myriah. "Barney's just a little snake. He can't hurt you. Besides, he could probably slither right up onto that chair. You can't escape him that way."

"Oh, EW!" shrieked Mary Anne.

"How did Barney get loose?" I asked her.

"Well, I'm not sure, but I think he just crawled out of his cage, or slithered out or whatever sn-snakes do. I — I mean, he did it after I forgot to put the lid back on his cage. I took it off so I could get a closer look at him, and then I heard someone saying, "Where's the beef? Where's the beef?" so I left to see who it was. And then I found the birds, and *then* I remembered Barney, and when I came back to replace the lid on his cage, he was gone. I am *so* sorry, Jessi."

"*Oh* . . ." I cried.

"Shouldn't we *find* Barney?" asked Myriah sensibly. "Before he gets too far away?"

"I guess so." I couldn't believe I was going to have to search for a snake. I couldn't think of anything stupider than searching for something you didn't want to find — or anything grosser than searching for a flicking tongue and a long, scaly body.

But it had to be done, and done fast.

"Let's split up," I suggested. "Barney probably couldn't have gotten upstairs, so we don't need to search there. Mary Anne, you and Gabbie look in the back rooms on this floor. Myriah and I will look in the front rooms."

"Okay," agreed Mary Anne, and we set off.

The search was a nightmare. Well, it was for Mary Anne and me. For Myriah and Gabbie it was like playing hide-and-seek with an animal. The odd thing was, I was so afraid of Barney that I was *less* worried about *not* finding him and having to tell the Mancusis he was lost than I was that we *would* find him. I went looking gingerly under chairs and tables and couches, always terrified that I'd come face to face with Barney and his flicking tongue.

But after twenty minutes of searching, there was no sign of Barney. And we'd been through every room on the first floor.

"Uh-oh," I said, as the four of us met in the hallway. "Now what? How am I going to tell the Mancusis that Barney is missing?"

"Long distance. It's the next best thing to being there!" called Frank from his cage.

We began to laugh, but then I said, "This is serious. We have to find Barney."

"Yeah," said Mary Anne. "Boy, am I sorry, Jessi. If — if you have to tell the Mancusis that . . . you know . . . I'll help you."

"Hey!" said Myriah suddenly. "I just thought of something. We're learning about animals in school, and Barney is a snake and snakes are reptiles and reptiles are cold-blooded. If I had cold blood, I'd want to warm up."

"Could Barney have gotten outside?" I said nervously. "Maybe he wanted sunshine. We might never find him outdoors, though."

"Well, let's look," said Mary Anne.

So we did. And we hadn't looked for long when Mary Anne let out another shriek.

"Where is he?" I cried, since I knew that was what her scream had meant.

"Here," she yelled. "On the back porch."

I ran around to the porch and there was Barney, napping peacefully in a patch of sunshine.

"You were right," I whispered to Myriah. "Thank you." Then I added, "How are we going to get him back in his cage, Mary Anne?"

Mary Anne looked thoughtful. "I have an idea," she said. "Do the Mancusis have a spare aquarium somewhere?"

I wasn't sure. We checked around and found one in the garage. It was empty but clean.

"Okay," said Mary Anne, "what we're going to do is put this aquarium over Barney. I'll — I'll do it, since I was the one who let him loose."

I didn't argue. The four of us returned to the porch, and Mary Anne crept up behind Barney, holding the overturned aquarium. She paused several feet from him. "I hope he doesn't wake up," she said.

Boy, I hoped he didn't, either.

Mary Anne tiptoed a few steps closer, then a few more steps closer. When she was about a foot away from him, she lowered the aquarium. Barney woke up — but not until the aquarium was in place.

"Now," said Mary Anne, "we slide a piece of really stiff cardboard under Barney. Then we carry him inside and dump him in his own cage. This is my spider-catching method. See, I don't like spiders, and I also don't like to squish them, so when I find one in the house, I trap it under a cup or a glass and take it outside."

Well, Mary Anne's suggestion was a good one. I found a piece of cardboard in a stack of newspapers the Mancusis were going to throw away. Mary Anne carefully slid it under Barney, the two of us carried him inside, Myriah opened his cage for us — and we dumped him in. I think Barney was relieved to be at home again.

Believe me, *I* was relieved to have him home. But if I'd known what was going to happen at our club meeting the next day, I would have thought that a snake on the loose was nothing at all.

CHAPTER 7

The Wednesday club meeting started off like most others, except that I actually arrived early! It was one of the first times ever. My work at the Mancusis' had gone quickly that day, and the dogs had behaved themselves, so I had reached Claudia's fifteen minutes before the meeting was to begin. I had even beaten Kristy.

"Hi, Claud!" I said when I entered her room.

"Hi, Jessi."

Claudia sounded sort of glum, but I didn't ask her about it. Her gloominess probably had something to do with the Kristy problem, and I wanted to stay out of that. So all I said was, "Neat shirt."

Claudia was wearing another of her great outfits. This one consisted of an oversized, short-sleeved cotton shirt with gigantic leaves printed all over it, green leggings — the same green as the leaves on her shirt — bright yellow push-down socks, her purple high-tops, and in her hair a headband with a gigantic purple bow attached to one side.

Claud is so, so cool . . . especially compared to me. I was also wearing an oversized shirt — a white sweat shirt with ballet shoes on the front — but with it I was just wearing jeans and regular socks and regular sneakers. And honestly, I would have to do something about my hair soon. It looks okay when it's pulled back, I guess, but I want it to look special.

I sat down on the floor. Since no one else had arrived, I guess I could have sat on the bed, but Mallory and I just don't feel comfortable doing that. We're the youngest and we belong on the floor. Period.

I was about to ask Claud if she'd printed the leaves on her shirt herself, when Dawn burst into the room.

"Hi, you guys!" she said cheerfully. She tossed her long hair over one shoulder.

"Hi," replied Claudia. "You're in a good mood."

"I'm thinking positive," Dawn informed us. "Maybe it'll help the meeting along. . . . I mean, I *know* it will help the meeting. This meeting," she went on, "is going to be wonderful. There aren't going to be any prob . . ."

Dawn's voice trailed off as Kristy strode into club headquarters. Without so much as a word, she crossed the room to Claudia's bulletin board, pulled out a few thumbtacks, and posted a piece of paper right over a bunch of photographs of Claudia and Stacey.

Kristy turned to us and smiled. "There!" she announced proudly, as if she had just achieved world peace.

"There what?" said Claudia darkly.

"There's the checklist. I made it last night. It took forev — "

"And you put it up over my *pictures?!*" exclaimed Claudia. "Not on your life. Those are pictures of Stacey and me before she moved away." Claudia marched to the bulletin board and took the checklist down. She gave it back to Kristy. "Find another place for this, Ms. Bossy."

"Sheesh, I'm *sorry*, Claud," said Kristy. "I didn't know those picture were so important to you."

"Well, they are."

Personally, I thought Claud was overreacting a little. I guess Kristy thought so, too. The next thing I knew, she was tacking the checklist up over the photos again.

Claudia yanked it off.

Kristy put it back up.

Claudia yanked it off again. This time, the

checklist ripped. From one side hung a wrin-
kled strip.

Mallory and Mary Anne arrived just in time
to hear Kristy let out a shriek and Claudia yell,
"Leave this thing *off!* I don't want it on my
bulletin board. I don't care how long it took
you to make it!"

"Girls?" The gentle voice of Mimi, Claudia's
grandmother, floated up the stairs. "Everything is okay?" (Mimi had a stroke last summer
and it affected her speech. Sometimes her
words get mixed up or come out funny.)

"YES!" Claudia shouted back, and I knew
she didn't mean to sound cross. She lowered
her voice. "Everything's fine, Mimi. Sorry
about the yelling."

"That okay. No problem."

Claudia and Kristy were standing nose-to-
nose by Claud's desk. They were both holding
onto the checklist, and I could tell that neither
planned to give it up. Not easily, anyway.

The rest of us were just gaping at them —
Mallory and Mary Anne from the doorway,
Dawn from the bed, and I from the floor.

"You," said Claudia to Kristy in a low voice,
"are not the boss of this club."

Kristy looked surprised. Even I felt a little
surprised. I don't think Kristy had meant to

be bossy. She was just overexcited about her checklist.

But Kristy retorted, "I am the *president* of this club."

"Then," said Claudia, "it's time for new elections."

"*New* elections?" Kristy and Mallory and I squeaked.

"Yes," said a voice from the doorway. "New elections." It was Mary Anne.

Claudia and Kristy were so taken aback that they both let go of the checklist. It fell to the floor, forgotten.

Everyone turned to look at Mary Anne.

And then Mallory spoke up. Even though she's only a junior officer of the club, she's known for having a cool head in tough situations. So she took charge. "Everybody sit down," she said quietly. "In your regular seats. We have some things to straighten out. And we better calm down in case the phone rings."

As if Mal were psychic, the phone did ring then. We managed to schedule a job for the Barrett kids. By the time that was done, we had settled into our places. Kristy, in the director's chair, had even put her visor on.

"Okay," she began, "a motion has been made for . . . for . . ."

"New elections," supplied Claudia.

"All right. I'll consider the idea," said Kristy.

"No way," said Dawn, who, since the checklist war, had barely said a word. "You can't just consider the idea. Elections are our right. I *demand* new elections."

"Me too," said Mary Anne.

"Me too," said Claudia.

Mallory and I exchanged a worried glance. We were certain to be asked our opinion soon. And we were still trying to remain neutral.

Sure enough, Kristy looked down at Mal and me. I cringed. I knew she wanted us on her side. If we were, then the club would be divided three against three.

"Mallory, Jessi, what do you two think about the elections?" Kristy asked.

It would have been awfully nice to side with Kristy. Siding with the president is always nice. But I just couldn't. I didn't want to get involved in a club fight. I knew Mal didn't, either.

Since Mal wasn't speaking, I finally said, "What do we think about the elections?"

"Yes," said Kristy sharply.

"I . . . Well, I . . ." I shrugged. Then I looked helplessly at Mal.

"I — That's how . . . um . . ." was all Mallory managed to say.

"Do you want them?" Mary Anne asked us.

"Not that your positions would change, but you'd be voting."

Mallory and I did some more stammering. I think both of us felt that elections were a good idea, but neither of us wanted to admit it. Furthermore, a new worry was already creeping into my worry-laden mind. *How* would Mal and I vote in an election? If we voted to keep Kristy president, all the other club members would hate us. If we voted Kristy out, Kristy would hate us, and whether she was the president or the secretary, the club was still hers because she had dreamed it up and started it.

"Jessi? Mallory?" said Kristy again. We didn't even bother to answer, and suddenly Kristy threw down the pencil she'd been holding and exclaimed, "Okay, okay, okay. We'll have an election." I guess she could tell that no one was on her side. Jessi and I might not have been on the *other* side, but we weren't on hers, either.

"Good," said Claudia. "Well, we're ready."

"Not *now!*" cried Kristy as the phone rang.

We scheduled three jobs, and then Kristy went on, "I don't want to waste one of our regular meetings on elections. Besides, people call all the time during meetings."

"They call plenty of other times, too," Claud couldn't resist saying.

"Whatever," said Kristy. "Anyway, I'm calling a special meeting for the elections. Saturday afternoon at four o'clock. *This* meeting is adjourned."

"Whew," I said to Mallory when we were safely outside. "I don't like the sound of this."

"Me neither," agreed Mallory. "Not at all."

CHAPTER 8

On Thursday, I had help at the Mancusis'. Mallory came over so we could discuss the election problem, and Becca came over so she could play with the animals. The night before, she'd been so excited about the trip to the Mancusis' that she practically couldn't sleep. Nevertheless, she was a big help that afternoon, and so was Mallory.

Becca and I reached the Mancusis' about fifteen minutes before Mal did. I wanted to walk the dogs before I began feeding the animals, so we would have to wait for Mal to arrive. I used the time to introduce Becca to the animals.

"Come on," I said to her. "Come see the birds. You'll love them."

"Just a sec," replied Becca. She was lying on the floor, playing with Ling-Ling and Crosby, who were enjoying every second of her attention.

When Becca finally got to her feet, I led her back to Frank. I was just about to say, "This is Frank. Listen to what he can do," when Frank said, "The quicker picker-upper! The quicker picker-upper!"

Becca began to giggle. "That's great! How'd he learn to do that?"

"Watched too much TV, I guess. Like some people I know," I teased my sister.

"Oh, Jessi," replied Becca, but she was smiling.

"Try saying, 'Where's the beef?' " I suggested.

"Me?"

I nodded.

"Okay." Becca stood directly in front of Frank and said clearly, "Where's the beef? Where's the beef?"

"Long distance," replied Frank.

Becca and I laughed so hard that we didn't hear Mallory ring the doorbell until she was leaning on it for the third time.

"Oh! That's Mal!" I cried. "I'll be right back, Becca."

I dashed to the door and let Mal in.

"What took you so long?" she asked cheerfully. (Mal is usually cheerful.) "I rang three times."

I explained about Frank, and then, of course,

I had to show him to her. I led her back to Becca and the birds, and Becca promptly said, "Hi, Mallory. Listen to this. Hey, Frank, where's the beef? Where's the beef?"

"The quicker picker-upper!" Frank answered.

When we had stopped laughing, I said, "Come on, you guys. We've got to walk the dogs. Cheryl looks sort of desperate."

I took the leashes from the hooks and before I could even call the dogs, they came bounding into the kitchen.

"Okay, you guys. Ready for a walk?" I asked. (Dumb question. They were *dying* for a walk.)

I snapped their leashes on and they pulled me to the front door. "Come on!" I called to Becca and Mallory, who were still talking to Frank. "The dogs can't wait!"

Becca and Mallory clattered after me. As we ran through the doorway and down the steps, Mal asked, "Can we help you walk them? We could each take one leash."

"Thanks," I replied, "but I better do it myself. Besides, they're used to being walked together. You can hold onto them while I lock the door, though."

So Mallory took the leashes from me while I locked the Mancusis' door. Then she handed them back, and we set off down the street —

at a fast pace, thanks to Cheryl and her very long legs.

"Keep your eye on Pooh Bear," I told Becca and Mal. "She's the troublemaker."

"The little one?" exclaimed Becca.

"Yup," I said. "For instance, up ahead is . . . Oh, no, it's a cat! For a moment I thought it was just a squirrel, but a cat's worse. Pooh Bear might — OOF!"

Pooh Bear had spotted the cat, who was sunning itself at the end of a driveway. She jerked forward with a little bark, straining at the leash. Jacques spotted the cat next, and then Cheryl, although Cheryl doesn't care about cats. Anyway, the cat heard the barking, woke up, saw the dogs, and fled down the driveway.

"*Hold* it, you guys!" I yelled to the dogs. Pooh Bear and Jacques were practically dragging me down the street. Cheryl, too. She always likes a good run.

"We'll help you, Jessi!" I heard my sister cry. A few moments later, she and Mallory grabbed me around the waist. They pulled back so hard that the dogs stopped short, and all of us — dogs, Mal, Becca, and I — fell to the ground. When us humans began to laugh, the dogs started licking our faces.

It took several minutes to sort ourselves out

and stop laughing, but finally we were on our feet and walking again. Things went smoothly after that.

"I never knew dog-walking was so hard," commented Becca.

"It's only hard when you're walking Pooh Bear, Jacques, and Cheryl," I told her. "And when they're in the mood for cat-chasing."

We returned to the Mancusis' and I let the dogs inside and hung their leashes up. "Okay," I said, "feeding time."

"Puh-*lease* can I feed some of the animals?" begged Becca. "Even though it's your job? I'll be really good and careful."

"We-ell . . . okay," I said, relenting. "You have to follow instructions exactly, though, okay?"

"Yes, yes, yes! Okay!" Becca was so excited she began jumping up and down.

"All right. You can feed the guinea pigs, the rabbits, and the cats. Let me show you what to do."

I gave Becca instructions, and then Mal came with me while I fed the other animals. I started with the dogs because they absolutely cannot wait, and they are gigantic pains when they're hungry.

"Well," said Mallory, as I spooned dog food

into Cheryl's dish, "What do you think about the elections?"

I groaned. "Please. Do we have to talk about them?"

"I think we better."

"I know. You're right. I was just trying to . . . I don't know what. Oh well. Hey, Mal, you're not thinking of quitting, are you?" The idea had just occurred to me and it was an awful one, but if Mal and I refused to take sides, would we feel forced to quit the club?

"Thinking of quitting?!" exclaimed Mal. "No way. No one's going to get rid of me *that* easily. . . . But the meetings *are* pretty uncomfortable."

"I'll say," I agreed.

"And how are we going to vote Saturday?" wondered Mallory.

"Well, I guess," I began slowly. "Let me think. Okay, there are four offices — president, vice-president, secretary, and treasurer. And you and I are going to remain junior officers, so it'll be the same four girls running for the same four offices."

"Right," agreed Mallory.

I finished feeding the dogs, rinsed off the spoon I'd used, changed the water in their bowls, and moved onto the bird cages.

"Yesterday I was thinking," I told Mallory, "that if we vote Kristy out of her office — if we make her secretary or something — she'll be mad at us, which won't be good. I mean, I'll always think of the club as hers, whether she's president or not, because it was her idea and she started it. And I don't want her mad at us. On the other hand, if we vote for Kristy for president, all the other girls will be mad at us, and that won't be good, either. It almost doesn't matter how we vote for Mary Anne and Dawn and Claudia, but where Kristy is concerned, we lose either way."

"Wait a sec," Mal cut in. "Won't the voting be secret?"

"It should be, but even if it is, everyone will figure out who voted for whom. People always do."

"Oh, brother," said Mallory. "You're right. *And* I just thought of something even worse. If enough feelings are hurt by the voting, the club could *break up*. It really could. Then what?"

"I don't know," I said, heading for the hamster cage. "I hadn't even thought of that."

Mal and I peered in at the hamsters.

"Do they always sleep in a pile?" asked Mallory.

"Pretty much," I replied. "Except for that one. I pointed to the one in the corner. "He sleeps by himself, and you know, I think he's fatter than he was a few days ago. I'm getting worried about him."

"Well, at least he's eating," said Mal.

"Maybe he's gotten too fat to move," I kidded, but I didn't try to smile at my joke. I was too worried. I was worried about the hamster, and worried about our special Saturday meeting.

Mal and Becca and I finished feeding the animals and changing their water. Becca played with the cats again and then it was time to leave.

"Good-bye, Cheryl! Good-bye, Ling-Ling!" Becca called. " 'Bye, Barney!' 'Bye, Fluffer-Nut!' 'Bye, Frank!' "

"Awk!" squawked Frank. "Tiny little tea leaves!"

Thursday

I always look forward to sitting for Jackie Rodowsky, our walking disaster, even though he's more of a challenge than almost any other kid I can think of. Today was a challenge as usual, but it was a different kind of challenge. Jackie's having a tough time -- and I tried to help him with his problem. I'm not sure I did, though. In fact, I think I might have been bossing him around. I mean, I guess I was bossing him. Have I always done that? Or is it just lately? Well, anyway, Jackie was nice about it.

Kristy *might* have been bossing Jackie around? I'll say she bossed him! The good thing is that I think she learned something from Jackie. Let me start back at the beginning of the afternoon, though, when Kristy first arrived at the Rodowskys'.

Ding-dong.

"Rowf! Rowf-rowf!" Bo, the Rodowskys' dog, skidded to a halt at the door and waited for someone to come open it so he could see who was on the other side. A moment later, the door was opened by Jackie himself.

"Hi, Kristy," he said gloomily.

"Good afternoon, Eeyore," Kristy replied with a smile.

"Huh?" said Jackie.

"You look like Eeyore. You know, the sad donkey from *Winnie-the-Pooh*."

"Oh."

"What's wrong?"

"I'll tell you later. Come on in."

Kristy stepped inside. She took a good look at Jackie's sad face. He's got this shock of red hair and a faceful of freckles. When he grins, you can see that he's missing teeth (he's only seven), so he looks a little like Alfred E. Neuman from *Mad* magazine. You know,

"What, me worry?" But not that day. Jackie wasn't smiling.

"My brothers are at their lessons," Jackie informed Kristy, "Dad's at work, and Mom's going to a meeting."

Kristy nodded. That often happens. Jackie doesn't take any lessons because he's too accident-prone. He's our walking disaster. When Jackie's around, things just seem to happen. Vases fall, dishes break, earrings disappear. Things happen to Jackie, too. *He* falls or breaks things or loses things. Which is why he doesn't take lessons anymore. He tried to, but there were too many accidents when he was around.

Mrs. Rodowsky came downstairs then, and Kristy greeted her and listened to her instructions for the afternoon. Then Mrs. Rodowsky kissed Jackie good-bye and left.

"So," said Kristy, "what's up, Jackie? You look like you have a big problem."

Jackie nodded. "Yeah. I do."

"Do you want to tell me about it? I don't know if I could help, but I might have a couple of suggestions."

"Well," Jackie answered, "I could tell you, I guess. That won't hurt anything."

"Shoot," said Kristy.

Jackie heaved a huge sigh.

"Wait, let's make ourselves comfortable." Kristy led Jackie into the rec room and they settled themselves on the couch, Bo between them.

"Okay," said Kristy.

"All right. See, in my class," Jackie began, "our teacher said we were going to have elections." (Elections? thought Kristy.) "There are all kinds of neat things you can run for — blackboard-washer, messenger, roll-taker."

"Sounds like fun," said Kristy.

Jackie nodded. "That's what I thought. I wanted to run for the job of taking care of Snowball. He's our rabbit. That sounded like the funnest job of all." Jackie stopped talking and stroked Bo behind his ears.

"But?" Kristy prompted him.

"But there's no way I'm going to win."

"How come?"

" 'Cause I'm running against Adrienne Garvey. Adrienne is . . . is . . ." Jackie paused, thinking. "Well, she never erases holes into her workbook pages, and she never gets dirty, even in art class. And she always finishes her work on time. And she never forgets her lunch or trips or spills or *any*thing!"

"Ms. Perfect?" Kristy suggested.

"*Yes*," said Jackie vehemently. "And all the

other kids will vote for her. I just know it. They don't like Adrienne very much, but they know she'll do a good job. She'll never forget Snowball, and she'll keep his cage neat and stuff."

"What about you?"

"Me?" replied Jackie. "You mean, what kind of job would I do?"

Kristy nodded.

"Just as good as Adrienne!" Jackie cried. "Honest. I take good care of Bo, don't I, Bo?" (Bo whined happily.) "But, see, Bo's not mine. I mean, not just mine. He belongs to my brothers *and* me, so I don't take care of him everyday. And Snowball wouldn't be mine, either. He belongs to the whole class. But if I got the job, he would *feel* like mine since I would be the only one taking care of him. And I know I could do a good job. I know it."

"Then prove it to the kids in your class," said Kristy. "Show them that you'll be as neat and as responsible as Adrienne. Maybe even neater."

"And responsibler?"

Kristy smiled. "That, too."

"But how am I going to show them that?" wondered Jackie.

"Well, let's think it over."

"I — I could be neat myself," said Jackie after a few moments, sitting up straighter.

"That's a good start."

"And I could try to keep my workbook neat. And my desk neat."

"Even better."

Jackie paused, frowning.

"Do you think you can do those things?" asked Kristy.

" 'Course I can!" To prove his point, Jackie jumped to his feet. "Watch me neaten up," he cried, and then added, "I did this once before, for a wedding. . . . Okay, buttons first." Jackie's shirt was buttoned wrong, so that on top an extra button stuck up under his chin, and on the bottom one shirttail trailed an inch or two below the other.

Jackie unfastened the first button — and it came off in his hands.

"Uh-oh," he said, but his usual cheerfulness was returning. "Um, Kristy, if you could . . . whoops." Another button came off.

"Here," said Kristy, "let me do that for you."

"No," said Jackie, "I have to learn to —"

Too late. Kristy was already unbuttoning and rebuttoning Jackie's shirt. "There you go," she said. "Now the next thing I think you should do is start a campaign—you know, slogans, speeches, that sort of thing."

"But I," Jackie replied, "think I should practice filling Bo's dish neatly. It's almost time to feed him anyway."

"Well," said Kristy reluctantly, "okay." She was thinking that she really wanted to help Jackie win the election for the job of Snowball-Feeder. But she was also thinking that Jackie plus a bag of dog food equals big trouble. However, if Jackie believed that feeding Bo would help him, then Kristy would go along with his idea.

"Where's Bo's food?" Kristy asked.

"It's — Oh, I just remembered. We used up a bag yesterday. We have to start a new one. Mom keeps them in the basement."

Kristy cringed. Jackie was going to carry a bag of dog food from the basement up to the rec room and then up to the kitchen? "Be careful," she called after him.

Jackie disappeared into the basement. A moment later, Kristy heard his feet on the stairs. "I'm coming!" Jackie announced. "And I'm being careful!"

Jackie reached the rec room safely.

He grinned at Kristy.

He headed up the stairs to the kitchen.

Halfway there, the bottom of the bag gave

out. Dog food cascaded down the stairs into the rec room.

Jackie looked at Kristy in horror. Then he smacked his forehead with the heel of his hand. "I did it again!" he exclaimed. His face began to crumple.

"Oh, Jackie," said Kristy, eyeing the mess. "Don't cry. It wasn't your fault." She wanted to reach out and give him a hug, but a sea of kibbles lay between them.

Jackie stood miserably on the steps. "I *know* it wasn't my fault," he cried.

"It couldn't have been," agreed Kristy. "The glue on the bottom of the bag must have come undone."

"But that's just it!" Jackie replied. "Don't you see? It came undone while *I* was holding it. Not Mom. Not Dad. Not my brothers. Not the man at the grocery store. Me. I'm bad luck. Maybe that's why the kids at school don't want me feeding Snowball."

"Then make the kids forget about your bad luck," suggested Kristy.

"How?"

"Campaigning. I'll help you with it as soon as we put this food into another bag."

"All right," said Jackie, but he didn't sound very enthusiastic.

Kristy found a garbage bag and the two of

them swept the kibbles into it. When nothing was left on the stairs but kibble dust, Kristy got out the Dustbuster.

"Let me do that," said Jackie.

"No, *I'll* do it." Kristy wasn't about to let Jackie touch an appliance. "Okay," she said a few minutes later, as she switched the Dustbuster off, "let's plan your campaign."

Jackie found a pencil and a pad of paper. He and Kristy sat down on the couch again, but Jackie immediately got up.

"Forgot to feed Bo," he said. "See? I am responsible. I remember to take care of animals." He ran upstairs, fed Bo, and returned to the couch without a single accident.

"All right," said Kristy, "now what I think you should do—"

"Kristy?" Jackie interrupted. "Can I tell you something?"

"Sure."

"I like you, but you're an awful bossy baby-sitter. You buttoned my shirt when I wanted to do it myself, you wouldn't let me vacuum up the mess I made, and now you're going to plan my campaign for — Whoops."

Jackie had dropped his pencil into a heating grate. He and Kristy had to scramble around in order to get it out. In the excitement, Jackie forgot about what he'd said to Kristy. But Kristy didn't. It was all she could think of later as she helped Jackie with his campaign — and tried very hard not to be too bossy.

Was she really a bossy person?

CHAPTER 10

I was scared to go to the Friday meeting of the Baby-sitters Club.

Isn't that silly? I really was afraid, though, so while I was at the Mancusis' feeding the animals and worrying about the hamster, I phoned Mal.

"Hi," I said. "It's me."

"Hi, Jessi. Where are you?"

"At the Mancusis'. I'm almost done, though. Um, I was wondering. You want me to come by your house so we can walk to the meeting together?"

"Are you scared, too?"

Now this is what I love about Mallory. I suppose it's why we're best friends. We know each other inside out, and we're always honest with each other. Mal knew I was scared. And she admitted that she was scared. She could easily just have said, "Are you scared?" but she said, "Are you scared, *too?*" which is very important.

"Yeah, I am," I told her.

"Well, *please* stop by. I'd feel much better."

So of course I stopped by. Mallory and I walked to Claudia's with our arms linked, as if we could fend off arguments and yelling and hurt feelings that way.

We had to unlink our arms at the Kishis' front door, though. It was the only way to get inside.

Mimi greeted us in the hallway.

"Who's here?" I asked her.

I must have looked scared because she answered, "All others. But do not worry, Jessi. I know plobrems will . . . will work out."

I nodded. "Thanks, Mimi."

Mal and I climbed the stairs as slowly and as miserably as if we were going to our own funerals. We walked down the hallway. I heard only silence. I threw a puzzled glance back to Mallory, who shrugged.

A few more seconds and I was standing in Claudia's doorway. Well, there was the reason for the silence. Everyone was present all right, but no one was talking — not to Kristy, not to each other.

Mary Anne was sitting stiffly on the end of

Claudia's bed. She was gazing at the ceiling; her eyes looked teary.

Claudia, at the other end of her bed, was leafing silently through one of her sketchbooks.

Dawn was seated between Mary Anne and Claudia, and her long hair was falling across her face, almost as if she hoped to hide from everyone by not being able to see them.

And Kristy, well, Kristy looked like she always looks. She was poised in the director's chair, her visor in place, a pencil over one ear. I couldn't read the expression on her face, though.

Oops, I thought, as I paused in the doorway. If I stand here too long, Kristy will say, "What's with you guys? Are you going to stand there all day? Come on in so we can get started."

But Kristy didn't say a word. She just glanced at Mal and me and gave us a little smile. So we crept into Claudia's room and settled ourselves on the floor.

Kristy waited another minute until the digital clock on Claud's desk read 5:30. That minute was the longest one of my life. I was dying to whisper something to Mal like, "This room feels like a morgue," or, "Calm down, everybody. You're too cheerful. You're going to get out of control." But I couldn't. For one thing, in all that silence, everyone would have heard what I said. For another, I think the girls kind of *wanted* to feel bad, and I wasn't about to be responsible for cheering them up.

"Order," said Kristy as the numbers on the clock switched from 5:29 to 5:30.

Everyone already was in order.

"Well, um, is there any club business?" asked Kristy.

No one said a word. No one even moved.

Since it wasn't Monday, there were no dues to be collected, and Kristy didn't need to ask if we'd read the notebook. (Not that she'd bring it up. I had a feeling "notebook" was going to be a dirty word for awhile.)

Kristy cleared her throat. "Well," she said in this falsely cheerful voice, "any snacks, Claud?"

Silently Claudia reached behind the pillows on her bed and pulled out a bag of Doritos and a bag of popcorn. She passed the Doritos to Dawn and the popcorn to Kristy. The bags circled the room in opposite directions. No one reached into the bags. No one took so much as a kernel of popcorn, not even Kristy, who had asked about food in the first place.

I guess that had just been something for Kristy to say, that she wasn't really hungry.

And that was when I realized that she — our president, our queen — was as uncomfortable as the rest of us were.

Ring, ring.

Thank heavens. A phone call. I had never been more relieved to hear that sound. Like robots, Dawn answered the phone and Mary Anne scheduled a job for Claudia with the Marshall girls.

Ring, ring.

Another call came in. Then another and another.

At about 5:50, the phone stopped ringing, and Kristy, looking more uncomfortable than ever, said, "All right. I — I have a few things to say about the elections tomorrow."

"We're still going to have them, aren't we?" asked Claudia.

"Of course. But I wanted to figure out a way to avoid ties in the voting. This is what I came up with. First of all, Jessi and Mallory, you'll be voting, as you know."

We nodded.

"There are two reasons for that," Kristy continued. "One, you're club members, so you *should* vote. Two, we need five people voting in order to prevent a lot of ties. I know that sounds confusing, but you'll see what I mean in a few minutes."

"Okay," Mal and I said at the same time.

"Next, the voting will be secret. I'll make up ballots with boxes by our names. All we'll have to do is write X's in the boxes. I don't think we can get much more secret than that."

Stony silence greeted Kristy. I frowned. Wasn't anyone else relieved to hear what she'd just said?

Kristy continued anyway. "The last thing," she said, "is that, you, Mary Anne, you, Claudia, you, Dawn, and I—the four of us—will be able to vote in the election for each office except the one we hold. In other words, I can vote in the elections for vice-president, secretary, and treasurer, but not president. The reason for this is that without me, for instance, five people will be choosing from among four people for president. A tie is possible, but not likely. I think we'll avoid a lot of revotes this way."

"Anything else?" asked Dawn from behind her hair.

"No, that about covers it."

"I'll say it does," snapped Claudia.

"What's that supposed to mean?" Kristy replied.

Yeah, I wondered. What *is* that supposed to mean?

"Can I answer?" spoke up Mary Anne. Her

voice was wobbling ever so slightly.

"Be my guest," said Claudia.

Mary Anne drew in a deep breath, probably to control her voice. "Kristy," she began, "have you ever heard of a democracy?"

Sensing an argument, Kristy replied sarcastically, "Why, no. I never have. What is a democracy, Mary Anne?"

Mary Anne tried hard to ignore the tone of Kristy's voice. "In a democracy," she said, "everyone has a say — "

"Which is why we're holding elections," Kristy interrupted, "and why we're all voting in them."

"I don't believe it," Dawn muttered. "She did it again."

"Kristy, would you listen to Mary Anne, please?" said Claudia.

Kristy rolled her eyes. Then she turned her gaze on Mary Anne and waited.

"In a democracy," Mary Anne began again, "everyone has a say in running the country. This club should be a democracy, too, Kristy, and the members should have a say in running things. In other words, you should have consulted us about the voting — about the ballots and the way the elections will be run."

Kristy blushed. I really thought she was going to apologize, but Dawn cut her off.

"But *nooooo*," Dawn said sarcastically. "You just barge ahead and do whatever seems right to you. You, you, you. You never think of what other people might want or feel."

It is not a good idea to make absolute statements like that — you *never*, *no one* does, *everybody* does. I have learned this the hard way. If I say to my mother, "But Mama, *everyone* is wearing them," she'll reply, "*Every*one? Your grandfather? Squirt?" You know, that sort of thing.

So naturally Kristy pounced on the "you never think" part of what Dawn had said. "I *never* think of other people? What about when Claudia broke her leg and wanted to quit the club. Didn't I help her through that? I even helped her figure out what was wrong. And what about — "

"But Kristy," said Mary Anne in a small voice, "so many times you just don't think. You just don't. . . " Mary Anne's wavery voice finally broke and she burst into tears.

Dawn jumped to her feet. "Oh, that is nice, Kristy. That is really nice. Now look what you did."

"Look what *I* did?! I didn't do that! Mary Anne cries all the time. She does it by herself."

Dawn didn't answer. She walked out of Claudia's room in a huff.

"Be back here at four o'clock tomorrow," Kristy shouted after her. She looked at the rest of us. "You, too," she added. "This meeting is adjourned."

Mary Anne didn't move from her place on the bed, and Claud edged toward her, looking sympathetic. Mallory and I waited for Kristy to leave. Then we left, too. We walked slowly down the stairs.

When we were outside, I said, "Well, was the meeting as bad as you thought it would be?"

"Yup," replied Mallory. "How about you?"

"Worse. It was worse. Do you have a good feeling about tomorrow?"

"Not really. Do you?"

"No. Well, 'bye, Mal."

"'Bye, Jessi."

CHAPTER 11

On Saturday morning I woke up with butterflies in my stomach. I felt just like I do on the morning of a dance recital. Nervous, nervous, nervous. What on earth would happen at the special meeting that afternoon? I lay in bed and worried.

It was funny. I'd only been living in Stoneybrook, Connecticut, for a few months, but the Baby-sitters Club had become extremely important to me. Maybe that was because it was the first place here, besides Mallory's house, where I'd felt completely accepted; where I'd felt it truly didn't matter that I'm black.

If the club were to break up — if the girls were to get so mad at each other that they decided not to continue it — what would happen? I knew I'd still have Mallory, and I knew I'd still be friendly with the other girls, but it wouldn't be the same. Not to mention that I *love* baby-sitting and I'd miss all the jobs I get through the club.

I heaved a deep sigh, trying to make the butterflies in my stomach calm down. I rolled over. At last I sat up. Maybe, I thought, if I stay in bed I can make time stop, and four o'clock will never arrive. Unfortunately, I'm too old to believe in things like that anymore.

I got out of bed, put some clothes on, and went downstairs. But I didn't go into the kitchen for breakfast. Instead, I checked my watch, decided it wasn't too early for a phone call, and dialed Mallory's number.

I sprawled on the couch in the den.

"Hello?" said a small voice on the other end of the phone.

"Hi . . . Claire?" (The voice sounded like Mallory's five-year-old-sister.)

"Yeah. Is this Jessi?"

"Yup. How are you?"

"Fine. I lost a tooth! And guess what — after *I* lost it, the *Tooth Fairy* lost it."

"She did? How do you know?"

"'Cause I found some money under my pillow and I found the tooth on the floor. The Tooth Fairy must have dropped it after she left the money."

I managed not to laugh. "I guess even the

Tooth Fairy makes mistakes," I said to Claire. "Listen, can I talk to Mallory, please?"

"Sure," answered Claire. "Mallory-silly-billy-goo-goo! Phone for you!"

A few moments later, I heard Mallory's voice. "Hello?"

"Hi, it's me."

"Hi, Jessi. How long did you have to talk to Claire?"

"Just for a few minutes."

"That's good. She's in one of her silly moods, in case you couldn't tell."

I laughed. Then, "So," I said, "are you ready for this afternoon?"

"I hope so."

"What do you think is going to happen?"

"You know, I really don't have any idea."

"Do you know who you're going to vote for?" I asked.

"I've been trying not to think about it," Mal told me. "And I tried so hard that I really haven't thought about it, and now I don't know who to vote for."

"Oh. I just don't know who to vote for, period."

Mal sighed.

I sighed.

"Well," I said finally, "I better get going. I

have a lot to do before the meeting. The Mancusis come home tomorrow, so today I want to make sure everything is perfect at their house. I've got to walk the dogs and feed the animals as usual, but I also want to clean out some of the cages, change the litter in the cats' box, that sort of thing."

"Okay. Will you come by for me again this afternoon? It'd be nice to walk to the meeting together," said Mallory.

"Sure," I replied. "I'll see you around quarter to four."

We said good-bye and hung up, and then I wandered into the kitchen, where I found my mother and Squirt. "'Morning," I said.

"'Morning, honey."

"Where are Daddy and Becca?"

"Your father went into the office for the morning, and Becca's gone over to Charlotte's house."

I nodded. I sat down in front of Squirt's high chair and made faces at him. "Mama?" I said after awhile.

My mother looked up from the recipe card she was reading. "Yes, honey? Aren't you going to eat breakfast this morning? Everyone else has eaten already."

"I'll eat," I replied, "but I have to ask you about something first."

Mama could tell it was important. She sat down next to me at the table. "What is it, honey?"

As best I could, I explained to her what was going on in the Baby-sitters Club. I told her everything — how Kristy can be bossy sometimes, that the other girls are upset, and what might happen at the elections that afternoon.

"Go-bler?" said Squirt from his high chair. He was playing with a set of plastic keys and two red rings.

"Jessi," said Mama, "I think you want me to tell you how to vote, don't you?"

"Well, yes," I answered. "I mean, even just a hint or something."

"But I can't give you answers. You have to make up your own mind. I will give you one piece of advice, though."

"Okay."

"Vote for the person you honestly think is best suited for each office. Don't worry about anything else."

"All right. Thanks, Mama."

I ate my breakfast, feeling somewhat let down. My mother always has the answers. Why couldn't she tell me who to vote for? But I knew there was no point in asking her again. I would just have to figure things out for myself, and I would have plenty of time to think while I worked at the Mancusis'.

The first thing I did was walk Pooh Bear, Cheryl, and Jacques. It was late morning and the dogs were frantic to get outside. I snapped their leashes on and led them to the front door. As soon as it was opened a crack, Pooh Bear pushed her way through. The dogs tried to bound across the front lawn while I was still trying to lock the Mancusis' door.

"Hold on!" I yelled.

I locked the door, and the dogs pulled me to the street. We took a wild walk, racing past people, bicycles, and mailboxes. At last the dogs slowed down, and I relaxed a little.

I decided to think about the elections. I would consider one office at a time, starting with treasurer. Dawn, I thought, made a good treasurer. She always collected our dues, she always remembered to pay Charlie, she always let us know when the treasury was getting low. But if she didn't like the job, then . . . well, Claudia certainly couldn't be treasurer. She's terrible at math. Mary Anne's okay at it, but she was so good as secretary. That left Kristy. Somehow, I just couldn't see her as treasurer of the Baby-sitters club.

This isn't getting me anywhere, I thought as I walked the dogs back to the Mancusis'.

I decided to try a different office. Vice-president. Claudia really was the perfect vice-president, what with her own phone and her own phone number. But, okay, she was tired of the job. So let's see. Kristy could be our vice-president, but how was she going to answer all the calls that come in at nonmeeting times? She couldn't. Not unless we moved club headquarters to her house. Maybe she could ask her mother and stepfather for her own phone. . . . That sounded like an awful lot of trouble to go to, just to switch offices in the club.

I couldn't solve that problem, so I put the election dilemma aside while I tended to the animals. I let the dogs back in the house and fed them. Then I changed their water. They ate quickly (and messily) and ran off. I cleaned up their area of the kitchen.

Then I moved on to the cats. Since they were in the living room, sleeping, I cleaned up their dishes and placemats first. I set their food out. I cleaned their litter box, found the Mancusis' Dustbuster, and vacuumed up the stray kitty litter that was strewn across the floor.

I worked very hard. I took care of the birds

and the bird cage, the rabbits and their hutch, and the fish and aquarium.

Time for the hamsters. I leaned over and peered into their cage. The fat one in the corner suddenly woke up and looked back at me with bright eyes.

"Why are you all alone?" I asked him. I stuck my finger in the cage, intending to stroke the hamster, but he lunged for me. I pulled my hand back just in time. "Whoa! What's wrong with you?" I exclaimed. I paused. I realized I had just said, "What's wrong with you?" A cold feeling washed over me. Something *was* wrong with the hamster. Maybe he had broken a bone. Maybe that's why he didn't want to be with the others and why he was bad-tempered.

Whatever was wrong had been wrong all week. It had been wrong since the Mancusis left, maybe even before that. The Mancusis hadn't noticed for some reason, but I had. I'd noticed right away. Why hadn't I done anything about it? What would the Mancusis think if they came back and I pointed out the hamster, saying he'd been sick or hurt all week, and then admitted that I hadn't done anything for him? That certainly wasn't very responsible. If I were baby-sitting and one of the kids got sick or broke a bone, I'd call his parents or his doctor or an ambulance. Well, I certainly wasn't going to call the Mancusis long distance about a maybe-sick hamster . . . but I could take the hamster to the vet.

I grabbed the phone and dialed my number. My mother answered.

"Mama!" I cried. "One of the hamsters is very sick. He sleeps in the corner by himself, and he's getting fatter and fatter, and just now he almost bit me. I think he might have a broken bone. Anyway, I noticed something was wrong last weekend and I don't know why I didn't do anything, but I didn't, and — "

"Jessi, honey, slow down," Mama broke in. "What do you want to do?"

"Take the hamster to the vet. Can you drive me?"

"Of course. Bring the address of the vet with you. And give me a few minutes to get Squirt ready. Your father's still at work. Oh, and please be careful with the hamster, especially since he's biting."

"Okay," I replied, calming down a little. "Thanks, Mama. You know which house is the Mancusis', don't you?"

Mama said she did, so we got off the phone. I was just about to figure out how we were going to take the hamster to the vet, when something occurred to me. I looked at my watch. Two-thirty. The special meeting of the Baby-sitters Club was supposed to start in an hour and a half.

I would never make it.

CHAPTER 12

I couldn't worry about the meeting, not just then, anyway. I had to get the hamster ready for the trip to the vet. What could I carry him in? I ran into the Mancusis' garage and found a stack of cardboard boxes. Among them was a shoe box. Perfect, I thought.

I filled the shoe box with shavings and carried it inside. Then I had to figure out how to get the hamster into the shoe box. I didn't want to touch him in case he was hurting. Finally I cleaned out an empty dog-food can, made sure there were no rough edges, placed some treats in it, put it in the hamster cage right next to the fat hamster — and he crawled in! Then I moved the can into the box. We were all set.

The hamster crawled back out of the can and quickly settled down in the box. He didn't try to get out. Even so, I punched some holes in the lid of the box, planning to bring it with me. You never know what might happen, so it's always best to be prepared.

Beep, beep.

That must be Mama, I thought.

I grabbed the box and my jacket and went outside, being careful not to jostle the box. The Mancusis' house key was in my pocket. I remembered to lock their front door.

"Thanks, Mama!" I cried, as I slid into the front seat of her car.

Behind me, Squirt was strapped into his car seat. He was babbling away.

"Let's see this little guy," said Mama.

I removed the lid and held out the box.

"He seems quiet," commented Mama, "but — "

"He's been just like this all week," I interrupted her.

"Okay, then. We better be on our way. Where's the Mancusis' vet?"

I gave her the address. Then I sat back. I felt relieved just to be doing something.

"Broo-broo-broo-broo," sang Squirt as we drove along.

We pulled into the parking lot of the veterinary offices, and I put the lid back on the box. No telling what we would find when we got inside. Well, it was a good thing I did. The waiting room was a madhouse. Mama stepped out of the car carrying Squirt and a bunch of his toys, and I stepped out with the hamster in the box. When I opened the door to the vet's office I was surprised. I'd never been to a vet because we've never had a pet, so I don't know what I thought the waiting room would be like, but . . .

For starters, it was noisy. Most of the people were sitting there with dogs or cats. The cats were safely in carrying cases, except for a Siamese on a leash. And they were fairly quiet, but two cats — the Siamese and a tabby cat — were yowling loudly. And plenty of the dogs were barking; the little ones with high, sharp yips, the big ones with deep rowfs.

Squirt looked around, taking in the people and animals, and listening to the noise, and his lower lip began to tremble.

Mama patted him on the back. It's okay, Mr. Squirt," she said. "It's just a lot of — "

Suddenly my mother let out a shriek. She pointed at something across the room. I looked and saw it, too.

It was a snake. And not just a little garter snake like Barney, either. Some great big kind of snake was draped around the neck of a boy who looked as if he were about fourteen years old.

"Oh, my . . ." my mother started to say.

She looked like she might faint, so I tried to

figure out how to catch both her and Squirt without squishing the hamster, if she did.

But she didn't. Thank goodness.

And from across the room the boy said politely, "Don't worry. He's just a boa constrictor. He's not poisonous or anything. Sorry he scared you."

My mother smiled at him, but headed for seats as far from the boy as possible. She sat Squirt safely in her lap. "All right, honey," she said to me, "you better go tell the receptionist about your hamster and explain why you don't have an appointment."

"Okay." I carried the hamster across the waiting room, skirting around the boy with the snake, and stepped up to the desk. I placed the box on the desk and opened it.

"Yes?" said the receptionist.

"Hi," I began. "My name is Jessi Ramsey. I'm pet-sitting for the Mancusis this week and one of their hamsters is sick."

"Oh, the Mancusis," said the woman. She seemed to remember the name. I realized that with all their animals, they must have to go to the vet fairly often. "What seems to be the trouble?"

"Well, it's just that he doesn't sleep with the other hamsters and he's very bad-tempered."

I edged the box forward and the woman peered in at the hamster.

"Fat, isn't he?" she commented.

"Yes," I replied. "In fact, he's fatter than he was a week ago. I think maybe he's in pain. Something just doesn't seem right."

The woman nodded. "Okay. If you're worried, it's better to have things checked out. I have to tell you, though, that because you don't have an appointment, and because this isn't an emergency, you might have a long wait. It's hard to tell. There are five doctors in today, which is a lot, but there are also a lot of animals waiting."

"That's okay," I told her. "Just as long as he gets checked." I started to stroke the hamster's head before I replaced the lid on the box, but thought better of it. Then I made my way back to Mama.

I was beginning to feel awfully nervous. I checked my watch. Two forty-five. A quarter to three. Our special meeting would start in a little over an hour. Could I possibly make it? Was there any way?

I sat down next to Mama and tried hard not to bite my nails.

Then Squirt leaned over from his place on Mama's lap and said, "Pockita?" which is his way of asking to play patty-cake. We played patty-cake until a girl about Becca's age came into the waiting room with her father. She was holding a kitten, and she headed for the empty seats next to Mama. Her father spoke to the receptionist.

"What an adorable kitten," said my mother as the girl settled herself in a seat.

Immediately the girl stood up again. "Her name is Igga-Bogga," she said. She offered Igga-Bogga to us, and Mama and I took turns holding her, while Squirt patted her.

Igga-Bogga was skinny. And she was pure white, not a patch or a stripe or even a hair of another color anywhere. If she were my cat, I would have named her Misty or Clouds or Creampuff.

I was about to mention those names to the girl, when she spoke up again. "Guess what. It's so sad. Igga-Bogga is deaf."

"Deaf!" I cried.

The girl nodded. "That happens sometimes with white cats."

Her father joined us and he and Mama began talking about white cats being deaf. I looked at my watch. Three-ten. Less than an hour until the special meeting. What could I do? The hamster was my responsibility, my sitting responsibility. If I were baby-sitting on a weekday afternoon and the parents didn't come home and I had a club meeting to go to — well, I'd just have to miss the meeting, wouldn't I? Sitting responsibilities come first. So right now, a sick hamster came first.

I knew I was right, yet I started tapping my fingers and jiggling my feet. Oh, I *hate* being late and missing events I'm supposed to go to, and I *especially* hate upsetting Kristy.

"Miss Ramsey?" It was the receptionist.

My head snapped up. "Yes," I said. "I'm right here."

I picked up the hamster and his box and got to my feet. Next to me, Mama gathered up Squirt and his toys.

I checked my watch for the umpteenth time. Three-thirty! How did it get to be three-thirty? I would have to call Kristy as soon as I could safely step out of the doctor's office.

A nurse led Mama and Squirt and me through a doorway, down a corridor, and into an examining room.

"Hi, there. I'm Doctor West," said a friendly looking man wearing a white lab coat. He stuck his hand out.

Mama and I shook it, and I introduced us.

"So you've got one of the Mancusi pets here?" said Dr. West when the introductions were over. "Let me take a look."

While Dr. West examined the hamster, I ducked into the waiting room to use the pay phone I'd seen there. First I called Kristy.

". . . so I'm not going to be able to make the meeting," I finished up after I'd told her the story. "I'm really sorry."

"No problem," Kristy replied easily. "You did the right thing."

"I did?" I said. "Even though it's a hamster?"

"The hamster is your sitting charge," said Kristy. "Pets, kids, it doesn't matter. You're being responsible. That's what matters."

"Thanks, Kristy."

"Listen, I'll call the others and tell them the meeting has been postponed. We'll try to arrange it for eleven o'clock tomorrow morning, but call me tonight to check on the time."

"Okay," I said. "Thanks again, Kristy."

I hung up the phone, then dropped in another coin and called Mal to explain why I wouldn't be stopping by her house to pick her up.

When that was done, I returned to Dr. West's office. I found him and my mother grinning.

"What?" I said. "Why are you smiling?"

"Because," answered Mama, "your hamster isn't a he, he's a she. And *she* is pregnant!"

"I'd say she's going to have her babies within the next twenty-four hours," added Dr. West.

"You were lucky you didn't touch her today. A pregnant hamster should not be handled." Dr. West instructed me to transfer the other hamsters to a separate cage so the mother could be alone with her babies after giving birth. "And don't handle her at all," he said again. "A pregnant hamster is very delicate. Put her back in her cage by lowering the box inside it and letting her crawl out."

"Okay," I replied. Then I thanked Dr. West.

I rode back to the Mancusis' in high spirits. "Just think," I said to Mama. "The hamster is a girl, not a boy, and she's going to have babies! I'll have to give her a name. I want to be able to call her something."

Mama dropped me off and Squirt waved to me from the car window."

"Good-bye!" I called. " 'Bye, Squirt. Thank you for helping me, Mama. I'll be home as soon as I walk the dogs again and do the afternoon chores."

Mama beeped the horn as she drove down the street.

I ran to the Mancusis' garage before I did anything else. There I found the aquarium we had used to capture Barney. I poured shavings into it and added some food and a spare water bottle, and gently moved the hamsters into it. Then, even more gently, I set the shoe box in

113

the old cage and let the pregnant hamster crawl out.

"What should I call you?" I asked aloud as she settled into her nest in the corner of the cage. "Maybe Suzanne. I always liked that name. . . . No. Suzanne is dumb for a hamster. Chipper? Nah, too cute. And it sounds like a boy's name. Sandy? You are sand-colored. Nah, that's boring. After lots of thinking, I decided to call her Misty, which is what I would name a white kitten if I had one. The hamster wasn't anywhere near white, but I decided that didn't matter. Misty was a good name.

I went home feeling excited. When I came back in the morning, Misty would be a mother!

CHAPTER 13

Sunday morning I woke up super-early. I had a lot to do at the Mancusis' before I left for Claudia's. I had to walk the dogs, feed the dogs and cats, and finish the chores I had begun the day before. And of course I wanted to check on Misty and her babies.

I ran straight for Misty as soon as I'd closed the Mancusis' door behind me. When I reached the kitchen, though, I slowed down and tiptoed inside. I peeked into Misty's cage.

Nothing.

Just Misty and her nest and a pile of shavings.

"Oh, you didn't have them yet," I said, feeling disappointed. I began to wonder if Dr. West had been wrong. Then what? Well, the Mancusis would be home in the afternoon. I would tell them the story and let them decide what to do. At least Misty had been to a doctor.

Besides, worrywart, I told myself, Dr. West said the babies would be born in the next twenty-four hours. There were about seven more hours to go until the twenty-four were up.

So I left Misty to herself, walked the dogs, fed them and the cats, finished the cleaning, and then . . . took off for our special club meeting. I dropped by Mallory's house on the way, since we were still planning to arrive at Claudia's together.

Mallory was waiting on her porch steps. "Hi!" she called when she spotted me.

"Hi," I replied.

Mallory ran across her front lawn. "Did the hamster have her babies yet?" she asked breathlessly. (I'd told Mal everything the night before.)

I shook my head. "Not yet. I wish she had. I wanted her to have them before the Mancusis get back."

"Maybe we could check on her after the meeting," suggested Mal.

"Oh! That's a good idea. We could *all* come."

Mal made a face at the thought, but the only thing she said was, "Do you know who you're going to vote for?"

I nodded my head slowly. "I think so. I probably won't know for sure until I'm actually voting, but right now I *think* I know."

"Funny," said Mal. "I feel the same way. . . .

Should we say who we're going to vote for?"

"No," I replied. "Better not. We should go ahead with what we've planned on. If we say anything, we might change each other's minds."

"Okay."

A few more minutes and Mal and I had reached the Kishis' house. We looked at each other.

"Dum da-dum dum," sang Mal ominously.

I laughed — or tried to.

Mal opened the door. We went inside and straight up to Claud's room. Kristy was already there, busily sorting through some slips of paper.

"Hi, you guys," Claud greeted us.

"Hi," we replied, settling into our places on the floor.

"What — " Claud started to say, but she was interrupted by the arrival of Mary Anne and Dawn, both looking a little sleepy.

When everyone was sitting in her usual spot, Kristy surprised us by beginning the meeting with, "Tell us about the hamster, Jessi."

I jerked to attention. I'd been preparing for the voting. Now I had to switch gears. "Well," I said, "this is good news. The hamster isn't sick — "

"Oh, that's wonderful!" cried Dawn. "So it was a false alarm?"

"Not exactly," I answered. "The hamster turns out to be a she. By the way, I'm calling her Misty for the time being. And Misty is . . . " (I looked at Mal, dragging out the suspense.)

"Yes?" shrieked Mary Anne.

" . . . Going to have babies!" I exclaimed. "Probably lots of them. Doctor West said hamsters usually give birth to six to twelve young. Those were his exact words. And it should happen any minute now, because yesterday afternoon he said it would happen within the next twenty-four hours."

"That is so exciting!" squealed Dawn.

"Babies!" exclaimed Mary Anne.

"Lots of them!" added Claudia.

"The Mancusis will be thrilled!" cried Kristy.

For a moment, I felt as if I were in a regular club meeting, back before we had started fighting all the time. Then Kristy said, "When the meeting is over, maybe we could go to the Mancusis' and see how Misty is doing." (Mal elbowed me.) "But right now," she went on, "we have a job to do."

I watched the faces of the other club members turn from happy and expectant to worried and uncertain.

Kristy organized the pile of papers before her into a neat stack. "Now," she said, "I've

118

made those special ballots, just like I said I would. Each piece of paper is headed with the name of one of the offices. Below that are the names of the four officers. All you have to do is make an X in the box by the name of the person you'd like to see in the office. Okay?"

The rest of us nodded our heads.

"Great," said Kristy. "Let's start with treasurer." She handed blank ballots to Mary Anne, Claudia, Mal, and me, and then gave one to herself.

"Everyone votes except Dawn," she reminded us.

Mary Anne raised her hand. "Uh, Kristy," she said timidly, "I'm — I'm really sorry, but I have to say something about that."

"Yeah?" replied Kristy.

"Well, it's just — it's just that, for instance, Dawn might not want to be the treasurer anymore, but maybe she's got a good idea about who the new treasurer should be. Who would know that better than Dawn? I understand what you said about ties, but I think we should *all* get to vote. If there's a tie, we'll have a revote. If we have to have too many revotes, then we'll think about letting only five people vote. But we should vote with six first."

I have to hand it to both Kristy and Mary

Anne. Kristy listened to Mary Anne's suggestion and took it seriously, and Mary Anne didn't cry.

"Okay," said Kristy, "let's vote on what Mary Anne said. Nothing fancy, just a show of hands. All those in favor of letting everyone vote in the elections, raise your hand."

Five hands went up. (Guess which one didn't?)

"Great. I guess we're all voting," said Kristy. "Luckily, I made extra ballots, in case of mistakes, so we're ready."

Kristy handed a ballot to Dawn. Then she gave each of us a blue ballpoint pen.

I looked at my ballot, my heart pounding. TREASURER was written across the top. Below it were the names Kristy, Claudia, Mary Anne, and Dawn. A box had been drawn to the left of each name.

I paused for a moment, but I knew what I was going to do. I picked up the pen and made an X next to Dawn's name. She was the best treasurer I could think of. But I was pretty sure she was going to kill me when she found out what I'd done (*if* she found out). The business of elections had started because the girls were tired of their old jobs and wanted a change. Well, too bad. I couldn't help that. Dawn was my choice for treasurer.

I glanced around Claudia's room and tried to measure the tension in the air. Funny, but there didn't seem to be much of it. The club members were busy voting, that was true, but more than that, no one was arguing. I think we were relieved that election day had finally come, no matter what it would bring.

When everyone had voted, we folded our papers in quarters and gave them back to Kristy, who carefully put them in a pile. Then she handed out the ballots for secretary, a few minutes later the ones for vice-president, and last of all, the ones for president. Each time, I voted quickly, knowing just what I had to do.

After the ballots for the office of president had been collected, Kristy said, "Let me just take a fast look through the ballots. If I see a lot of problems, I'll ask you guys to help me count."

Kristy picked up the ballots for treasurer and glanced at them.

"Hmm," she said.

She looked at the ballots for secretary.

"Huh," she said.

She looked at the ballots for vice-president.

"Well," she said,

And then she looked at the ballots for president.

She burst out laughing.

"What *is* it?" cried Claudia.

"You will not believe this," Kristy told us. "I hardly believe it myself."

"But?" Dawn prompted her.

"But we unanimously voted ourselves back into our old offices! We all voted for Dawn for treasurer — even Dawn did. We all voted for Mary Anne for secretary — even Mary Anne did. And so on. You guys even voted for me for president."

There was a moment of silence. Then every single one of us began to laugh. Dawn laughed so hard she cried. Kristy laughed so hard I thought she was going to fall out of the director's chair. And all the time we were laughing I was thinking. Now I understand what Mama meant when I asked her to tell me how to vote. She meant (but wanted me to figure out for myself) that we shouldn't worry about who thought what or who would be mad or who would laugh about our choices. The purpose of an election is to vote the best person into an office. Period. And we realized that. We realized that the best people were already *in* the offices and we wanted to keep them there.

The laughter was fading, and Kristy straightened up in her chair. "What happened?" she asked us.

I raised my hand, heart pounding. I usually

don't speak up much in meetings, but I was pretty sure I had the right answer this time. "I think," I began, "that we realized the best people had already been elected to the offices. I mean, Dawn is organized, but Mary Anne is even more organized, and Dawn is better at keeping figures straight, so Dawn's the perfect treasurer and Mary Anne's the perfect secretary. It would be tough to name anyone but Claudia as vice-president, and Kristy, you really deserve to be president since the club *was* your idea."

Everyone was looking at me and nodding. I added one more thing. "Can you live with the results of the election?" I asked the four officers. "You were pretty fed up with your jobs a little while ago."

"I can do it," said Dawn quickly, and the others agreed. "There are parts of my job that I don't like, but I guess I know I'm best at this job. And it would really mess up the club to start switching things around."

My friends were smiling again. Then Kristy's smile faded. "I have something to say," she began. "Okay, we realized we were in the right offices. But I have to admit that right office or not, I have been too bossy. Maybe I do come up with good ideas, but I shouldn't force them on you. It's — it's just this thing with Charlie, I guess. You know something? I don't think he's acting like a big shot because he'll be in college. I think he's worried that he won't get into college, and he's taking his worries out by bossing me around. Then I take things out by bossing everyone else around. Jackie Rodowsky pointed that out to me. I mean, he pointed out that I was bossing him around. So I'm going to try to be better. No more forcing rules on you guys. When I get a new idea we'll vote on it, okay?''

"All *right!*" cried Claudia.

So the meeting ended happily. And when Kristy suggested again that we go over to the Mancusis', everyone wanted to see Misty. And Mal didn't mind. She was glad our club was a club again.

So was I.

CHAPTER 14

We arrived at the Mancusis' just before twelve-thirty. Mr. and Mrs. Mancusi wouldn't be home until later in the afternoon.

I unlocked the front door, feeling like a nervous grandmother. How was Misty doing? Had she had her babies yet? How long did a hamster take to have babies anyway?

"Follow me," I said. "Misty's in the kitchen." (For some reason I was whispering.)

I tiptoed into the kitchen, and Mal, Kristy, Claudia, Dawn, and Mary Anne tiptoed after me. I paused in the doorway, listening for unusual sounds, although what sounds a baby hamster might make I cannot imagine.

At last I looked into Misty's cage. There she was, a golden brown body. . . . And there were four tiny pink bodies! They looked like jelly beans. They had no hair at all and their eyes were closed.

I gasped. "She's had them!" I whispered. "Misty had four babies!"

Everyone crowded around the cage.

"Make that five," said Kristy softly.

"Oh, EW!" exclaimed Mary Anne, backing away. "That is disgusting."

"No, it isn't. It's beautiful," said Dawn.

"Five babies. I wonder what the Mancusis will name them," said Mal. "I wonder if there will be more than five."

"*I* wonder if they'll keep them," said Claudia. "Do you think they will, Jessi?"

I shrugged. "I don't think another cageful of hamsters would be much extra work."

"Is there anything we're supposed to be doing for Misty or her babies?" asked Mary Anne, even though she wouldn't look in the cage anymore.

"I don't think so," I replied. "Doctor West said to be sure not to touch the babies, even if I think one is dead. He said Misty will know what to do. He said the babies — actually he called them pups — will get scattered all around the cage, but that Misty will take care of them."

We watched for a few more minutes. Finally I said, "Maybe we should leave Misty alone. If I were in a cage giving birth to hamsters, I wouldn't want six faces staring at me."

"If you were in a cage giving birth to ham-

126

sters," said Mal, "you'd be a miracle of science."

"No, she'd be in a zoo!" said Kristy.

We left the kitchen and wandered into the living room.

"Aw," said Claudia, "who's this guy?"

"That's Powder. Hey, do you want to meet the rest of the Mancusis' animals? I mean, do all of you want to meet them?"

"Thanks, but I've already met Barney," Mary Anne replied drily.

"There are other animals here, though, and Kristy and Dawn haven't been over before. Also — "

"Where's the beef? Where's the beef?"

"Aughh!" shrieked Kristy. "Someone's in the house! We're not alone!"

Dawn began to laugh. "It's a bird, isn't it?" I nodded.

"We used to have one," Dawn told us. "A long time ago. I think it was a parakeet. His name was Buzz. He could say a few words. But the funniest thing he ever did was fly into a bowl of mashed potatoes."

"Dawn!" I exclaimed. "Is that true?"

"Cross my heart," she replied.

It must have been true.

We were all laughing hysterically and couldn't calm down for awhile. When we finally did, we checked on Misty (six babies) and then I let Kristy and Dawn meet the animals.

"Hey, Mary Anne!" called Kristy as we were leaving the sun porch. "Where's the lid to Barney's cage?"

Mary Anne began screaming without even turning around to look at the cage. If she had turned around, she would have seen that the lid was on tightly. Kristy had to confess her joke in order to keep Mary Anne from running home.

At last I suggested that we take Cheryl, Jacques, and Pooh Bear on their afternoon walk. I thought my friends might enjoy that.

So we took the dogs on a long walk. When we returned I said, "Well, you guys, I hate to kick you out, but I have to feed the animals. And I should probably be the only one here when the Mancusis come home."

"Okay," Kristy answered. "We understand."

My friends left. I was alone in the house, although not for long. The Mancusis would return soon. Even so, I phoned my parents to tell them where I was and why I'd be late. Then I looked in on Misty. *Ten* pups! And they were all gathered around their mother in a big jumbly pile of legs and feet and ears. I guess

Misty had finished giving birth. Now she could tend to her babies.

While I waited for the Mancusis, I found a roll of crepe paper (out in the garage, with all the boxes) and tied a big red bow to each of the dogs' collars.

"You three look lovely," I told them. "You're doggie fashion plates."

"Rowf?" asked Jacques, cocking his head.

"Yes, you're very handsome."

I was about to make bows for the cats when I heard a car pull into the driveway. "Guess who's home!" I called to the dogs.

Of course, they had no idea, but when I ran to the front door, they followed me. I opened the inside door and waved to Mr. and Mrs. Mancusi as they unloaded their luggage from the car. They were surprised to see me, but they smiled and waved back. Then, their arms weighed down with suitcases, they walked to the front door, while I tried to open it for them and hold the dogs back at the same time. It wasn't easy, but we managed.

As soon as the Mancusis were safely inside, I cried, "Guess what! One of the hamsters had babies! . . . Oh, I hope you had a nice vacation."

"My heavens!" exclaimed Mrs. Mancusi.

"One of the hamsters had babies?! How could we have missed a pregnancy? Are the babies okay? Which hamster is it?"

"Everything's fine. Honest," I told them. "I knew something was wrong, well, I knew something was *unusual,* so my mom drove the hamster and me to your vet yesterday. Dr. West looked at her and he told me what to do."

"Oh. . . ." The Mancusis let out a sigh of relief.

"Do you want to see the babies?" I asked.

"Of course," said Mr. Mancusi. He and his wife put down their suitcases and followed me into the kitchen, the dogs bounding joyfully at our sides.

"It's this one," I said. "I moved the other hamsters to the aquarium on the table." I stood back so the Mancusis could look in at Misty.

"Ah, Snicklefritz." Mrs. Mancusi scratched her head. "How did we miss this? I really apologize, Jessi. But I have to congratulate you. You did a terrific job in a difficult situation. We're very grateful to you."

"I guess," added Mr. Mancusi, "that in the excitement when we were trying to get away — our pet-sitter canceling and all — we just didn't notice that Snicklefritz was pregnant."

"Well, everything worked out fine," I spoke

up. "Mis — I mean, Snicklefritz has ten babies."

The Mancusis watched them for a few moments. Then they turned to me. "Thank you again, Jessi," said Mr. Mancusi. "You've been very responsible." He handed me some money — much more than I've gotten paid for any other job.

"Wow!" I cried. "Thanks. . . . Are you sure this isn't too much?"

"Not at all."

"By the way," said Mrs. Mancusi, "do you have any friends who would like a hamster? We'll let the babies go to anyone who will give them good homes — in about three weeks, that is. After the pups are weaned."

"*Any*one?" I repeated. "Gosh, we've never had a pet. I'm sure my sister Becca would like one. *I'd* like one. And, well, I'll spread the word. I bet I can help you find lots of homes!"

I couldn't believe it. A pet! Would Mama and Daddy let us have one? I had no idea. Neither Becca nor I had ever asked for a pet.

I headed for the front door. The dogs followed me.

"Good-bye, Cheryl. Good-bye, Jacques. Good-bye, Pooh Bear," I said.

The Mancusis were right behind the dogs. "They really like you," Mr. Mancusi said. "Oh, and *we* like their bows. Very spiffy."

I smiled. "Well, thanks again. If you ever need another pet-sitter, let me know. And I'll find out about homes for the baby hamsters. I promise."

The Mancusis and I called good-bye to each other and then I ran to my house. I was just about bursting with my news — Snicklefritz's babies and homes for them. Maybe one would become our first pet.

"Mama! Daddy!" I shouted as I burst through our front door.

CHAPTER 15

The Braddocks were back. Ballet school was in session again. My life had returned to normal.

I missed the Mancusi animals, but I could probably visit them any time I wanted to. I'm sure I'd be allowed to walk the dogs from time to time.

Anyway, since my life was back to normal, I baby-sat for the Braddocks the next day, Monday, and then tore over to Claudia's house. I reached it a full five minutes before the meeting was supposed to start. I even beat Kristy, but of course she's at the mercy of Charlie, so she doesn't have a lot of control over when she arrives.

Claudia and Dawn were there, though.

"Hi, you guys!" I said as I entered Claud's room.

"Hello," they replied, smiling, and Dawn added, "You sound awfully happy."

"Glad to be back at the Braddocks'?" asked Claudia.

"Yes," I answered, "but it's more than that. I'll tell you all about it when everybody's here."

"Okay," said Claud. "Potato chips, anyone?"

"Oh, I'm starving!" I exclaimed, even though I sort of watch my diet because I have to stay in good shape for dance class.

"Um, can you help me find them?" asked Claud, looking puzzled. "They might be under the bed, but who knows?"

Claudia and Dawn and I dropped to our stomachs and crawled halfway under Claud's bed. A ton of junk had been stashed there — boxes of art supplies, folders of drawings and sketches, magazines for making collages, that sort of thing. And because Claudia is such a poor speller, they were labeled SKECHES or PANTINGS or BURSHES.

I found the potato chips in a box marked CALAGE SUPPLIES.

"Here they are!" I announced.

The three of us crawled out from under the bed, stood up, turned around, and found Kristy, Mallory, and Mary Anne staring at us. We began to laugh — all six of us.

"That was so attractive!" said Kristy. "I hope

I always come to a meeting just in time to see the three of you backing out from under a bed."

"My backside is my best side," replied Dawn, looking serious.

There was more laughter as the members of the Baby-sitters Club settled into their usual places. Kristy climbed into the director's chair. She put her visor on. She stuck a pencil over one ear.

And then she pulled a new checklist out of her pocket, smoothed the creases, and with big, showy sweeps of her arms, tacked it up on the bulletin board over the photos of Claudia and Stacey.

"There," she said with satisfaction.

Claudia, Mary Anne, Dawn, Mallory, and I just stared at her. I guess my mouth was hanging open. Everybody else's was.

"I don't believe it," muttered Claudia, but just when it looked like she might jump to her feet and strangle Kristy, Kristy jumped to *her* feet and ripped the checklist off the bulletin board.

"Now watch this, everyone," she announced. She scrunched up the checklist and threw it in the wastebasket. "'Bye-bye, checklist. That's the last of it. You won't see it or hear about it again."

At first the rest of us didn't know what to do. Then we began to smile.

"You mean that was a joke?" exclaimed Claudia. "Oh, my lord! *Kristy* . . ."

Kristy grinned at us. She looked like the Cheshire Cat reclining in his tree.

Dawn threw a potato chip at her. I think a potato chip war might have started if the phone hadn't rung.

"Oh, no! We haven't done any of our opening business!" cried Kristy. "Dawn hasn't collected dues, I haven't — "

Ring, ring.

Kristy stopped ranting and raving and answered the phone. "Hello, Baby-sitters Club."

We arranged a Saturday afternoon job for me with the Arnold twins. Then Kristy got down to business.

"Dawn?" she said. "Ms. Treasurer?"

"I need your dues," announced Dawn.

Dawn collected the dues while we groaned and complained. "I'll walk out with you after the meeting and pay Charlie," she told Kristy.

"Okay. Thanks. That'll be fine. Maybe that will improve Charlie's mood." Kristy paused. "All right," she continued, "any club business?"

"I have something to ask everyone," I said,

"but it can wait until after the real club business is over."

Kristy nodded. "Anything else?"

The rest of the girls shook their heads.

"Okay," said Kristy. "I'm done. Over to you, Jessi. Oh, by the way, did you all notice that I didn't ask whether you'd read the notebook?"

"Uh, yes," replied Dawn.

"Good. I'm not going to ask anymore. I'll trust you to read it. No questions, no checklists — "

"You'll actually trust us?" exclaimed Mary Anne.

"I'll actually trust you."

The phone rang again, and we arranged another job. When that was taken care of, I said, "Well, guess what. Misty's name turns out to be Snicklefritz and she had *ten* pups yesterday." (Mallory knew this already, since we tell each other everything. But the others hadn't heard.)

"Ten pups!" cried Mary Anne. "What will the Mancusis do with them?"

"Well, that's the rest of my news. The Mancusis are giving them away — to anyone who'll promise the babies a good home. *And* Mama and Daddy said Becca and I can have one! Our first pet! We decided to name our hamster Misty no matter what color it is, and whether it's a boy or a girl."

"Oh, that's great!" cried Mary Anne and Kristy at the same time. (They both have pets.)

"And," I went on, "I'm asking around, finding out if anyone else would like a hamster. How about one of you?"

Claudia shook her head. "They're cute, but I hate cleaning cages."

Mary Anne shook her head. "A hamster wouldn't last a second around Tigger."

Kristy shook her head. "We've got enough pets at our house already."

Dawn shook her head. "I like hamsters, but if I get a pet, I'd like a bigger one. A cat or a dog."

I looked at Mallory. She seemed thoughtful. "We've got ten people in our family," she said slowly, "but no pets. I don't see why we couldn't get one little pet. The younger kids would like a hamster. So would the boys. Well, so would all of us." Mallory dove for the phone. "Mom! Mom!" she cried.

(I could just imagine Mrs. Pike saying, "What on earth is the matter?")

"Mom, the Mancusis are going to give the hamster babies away. In about three weeks, I think." (I nodded.) "Could we have one? It would be a good experience for Claire and Margo. And I think Nicky would like a pet . . . Yeah? . . . I know . . . Okay . . . Okay, thanks! This is great! 'Bye, Mom." Mallory hung up. "We can have one!" she announced. "We'll be getting our first pet, too!"

I have never seen so much excitement.

Then the phone rang and we lined up three jobs.

When the phone rang a fourth time, Mary Anne opened the record book again, and we sat up eagerly. I picked up the receiver. "Hello, Baby-sitters Club," I said.

"Hi," answered a very small voice. "I —This is Jackie Rodowsky. Is Kristy there, please?"

"Sure, Jackie. Hold on," I told him.

I handed the phone to Kristy, whispering, "It's Jackie Rodowsky."

Kristy raised her eyebrows. "Hi, Jackie."

That was all she said, and Jackie burst into tears.

"What's wrong?" she asked him. "What happened? Is your mom home?"

"She's here," Jackie told her. "And I'm okay. I mean, I'm not hurt. But we had our class elections today."

"Oh," said Kristy. "Right. And what happened?"

"I lost. Adrienne beat me. I tried and tried

to show the kids that I could take care of Snowball. But I don't think they believed me." Jackie paused. When he started speaking again, his voice was trembling. "I just — just wanted a pet to take care of by myself. That's all."

"Jackie," said Kristy gently, "I'm sorry you lost. I'm sorry the kids wouldn't pay attention to you. Really I am. Sometimes things just work out that way. But listen, could I talk to your mom for a sec, please?" There was a pause while Kristy waited for Mrs. Rodowsky to get on the phone. Then she said, "Hi, Mrs. Rodowsky. This is Kristy Thomas. Jackie told me about the elections today and I was wondering — could he have a pet of his own? I think he wants one, and I know where he could get a free hamster. . . . Yes. . . . Really? Oh, terrific! Could I talk to Jackie again, please?"

So Kristy gave Jackie the good news about his hamster.

"My own? My own hamster?" Jackie shrieked. "Amazing! What will I name it? Is it a boy or a girl? What color is it?"

Kristy couldn't answer his questions, so we arranged for me to take him over to the Mancusis' in a couple of weeks. The hamsters wouldn't be ready to leave their mother yet, but Jackie could look at them and pet them and play with them in order to choose the one that would become his very own. Jackie liked the idea a lot. So he thanked Kristy eleven times and then they got off the phone.

"Well, all's well that ends well," said Kristy.

"Huh?" said Claudia.

"I mean, happy endings everywhere you look. We got our club problems straightened out. The sick hamster turned out to be pregnant, and then she had her babies and they were born without any trouble, and now Jessi and Mallory's families will have their first pets, and Jackie lost the election but he got a hamster. Happy endings."

"Yeah," I said, smiling.

The numbers on Claudia's digital clock turned from 5:59 to 6:00.

"Meeting adjourned," announced our president.

I walked out with Mal. "I wonder," I said, "if I could talk Becca into changing Misty's name to Mancusi."

"Darn!" said Mallory. "That's what I wanted to name our hamster."

"Really?"

"Nah."

We giggled.

"Call you tonight!" I shouted to Mal as we separated.

Best friends have to talk a lot.

About the Author

ANN M. MARTIN did *a lot* of baby-sitting when she was growing up in Princeton, New Jersey. Now her favorite baby-sitting charge is her cat, Mouse, who lives with her in her Manhattan apartment.

Ann Martin's Apple Paperbacks are *Bummer Summer*, *Inside Out*, *Stage Fright*, *Me and Katie (the Pest)*, and all the other books in the Baby-sitters Club series.

She is a former editor of books for children, and was graduated from Smith College. She likes ice cream, the beach, and *I Love Lucy*; and she hates to cook.

Look for #23

DAWN ON THE COAST

Since no phone calls were coming in for the We ♡ Kids Club, we just sat around chatting. Jill and Maggie talked some more about the kids I remembered in our class. Right then an idea began taking seed in my mind. I started to picture myself back in the class, and how easy it would be to slip right back in.

Sunny came back up with the food — guacamole dip and cut-up raw vegetables that she had made earlier in the afternoon.

"All *right*," Jill said, grabbing a carrot stick.

"No calls yet?" Sunny asked.

We shook our heads. The phone hadn't rung once.

Sunny chomped on a celery stick and looked at me.

"It'd be great if you can stay for dinner," she said.

I thought back to all the times in the past that I had had dinner over at Sunny's house.

143

How many times had it been? Probably a thousand. Well, at least a hundred. Sunny's mom and dad were great. When we were younger they always let us be excused from the table as soon as we had finished eating, just so we would have a longer time to play.

"I hope you can stay," Sunny said again, and suddenly something popped into my head.

Maybe I *could* stay. Maybe I could *really* stay. Maybe I didn't have to go back to Connecticut at all, or just go back to get my things. Maybe I could move back in with Dad and Jeff, have my old room back, my old friends, my old school.

It was a strange thought, scary and exciting at the same time. Until then, I had just been having a great time, a *fabulous* time, but it had never occurred to me that I could think about making it last forever (or at least for longer). Now that the thought occurred to me, what was I supposed to do?

**Here's some news about other books
in The Baby-sitters Club series
by Ann M. Martin**

#1 *Kristy's Great Idea*

Kristy thinks the Baby-sitters Club is a great idea. She and her friends Claudia, Stacey, and Mary Anne all love taking care of kids. But nobody counted on crank calls, wild pets, and uncontrollable two-year-olds! Having a Baby-sitters Club isn't easy, but Kristy and her friends won't give up till they get it right!

#2 *Claudia and the Phantom Phone Calls*

Claudia has been getting some mysterious phone calls when she's out baby-sitting. Could they be from the Phantom Jewel Thief who's operating in the area? Claudia has always liked *reading* mysteries, but she doesn't like it when they *happen* to her!

#3 *The Truth About Stacey*

The truth about Stacey is her parents want to find a miracle cure for her diabetes. They're making Stacey's life so hard! The other Baby-sitters are busy fighting the Baby-sitters Agency. How can they help Stacey and save the club, too?

#4 Mary Anne Saves the Day

Mary Anne's never been a leader of the Baby-sitters Club. Now there's a big fight among the four friends. It's bad enough when Mary Anne has to eat at the lunch table all alone. But when she has to baby-sit a sick child with no help from her friends — it's time to take charge!

#5 Dawn and the Impossible Three

Poor Dawn! It's not easy being the newest member of the Baby-sitters Club. She's got three impossible kids to take care of. And Kristy thinks things were better *without* Dawn around. It'll take a lot of work to make things run smoothly again, but Dawn's up to the challenge!

#6 Kristy's Big Day

It's a big day for Kristy, all right — she's a bridesmaid in her mother's wedding! And if that's not enough, she and the other Baby-sitters Club members have *fourteen* wedding-guest kids to take care of. Only the Baby-sitters Club could cope with this one!

#7 Claudia and Mean Janine

This summer the Baby-sitters Club is starting a play group in the neighborhood. Claudia can't wait for it to begin — it'll give her some time away from her mean big sister. But then her grandmother has a stroke . . . and the whole summer changes.

#8 Boy-Crazy Stacey

Who needs baby-sitting when there are boys around? Stacey and Mary Anne are mother's helpers at the Jersey shore, and Stacey's mind is on hunky lifeguard Scott. Mary Anne's doing the work of two baby-sitters . . . but how can she tell Stacey that Scott's too old, without breaking Stacey's heart?

#9 The Ghost at Dawn's House

Creaking stairs, noises behind the wall, a secret passage — there must be a ghost at Dawn's house! The Baby-sitters find themselves and one of their charges wrapped up in a mystery. Will they be able to solve it?

#10 Logan Likes Mary Anne!

Quiet, shy Mary Anne has been growing up lately . . . and the Baby-sitters aren't the only ones who've noticed. Logan Bruno likes Mary Anne! He has a dreamy southern accent, he's awfully cute — and he wants to join the Baby-sitters Club. Life in the club has never been this complicated — or this fun!

#11 Kristy and the Snobs

The kids in Kristy's new neighborhood aren't very friendly. In fact they're . . . well, snobs. They laugh at everything — even Kristy's poor old collie, Louie. Kristy's fighting mad. But if anyone can beat a Snob attack, it's the Baby-sitters club. And that's just what they're going to do!

#12 Claudia and the New Girl

Claudia really likes Ashley, the new girl at school. Ashley's the only one who takes Claudia seriously. Soon, Claudia's spending so much time with Ashley that she doesn't have time for baby-sitting — or her old friends. And they don't like it one bit!

#13 Good-bye Stacey, Good-bye

There are lots of tears when the Baby-sitters hear the news: Stacey and her family are moving back to New York. The club members can't think of a special enough way to send Stacey off. They want to give her much more than a party. But how do you say good-bye to your best friend?

#14 Hello, Mallory

Mallory Pike has always been good at baby-sitting her younger brothers and sisters. But is she good enough to join the Baby-sitters Club? The club members go overboard giving Mallory baby-sitting tests. Mallory's getting pretty fed up. . . . Maybe she'll just start a baby-sitting business of her own!

#15 Little Miss Stoneybrook . . . and Dawn

Mrs. Pike wants Dawn to help prepare Margo and Claire for the Little Miss Stoneybrook contest. And Dawn wants her charges to win! The only trouble is . . . Kristy, Mary Anne, and Claudia are helping Karen, Myriah, and Charlotte enter the contest, too. And nobody's sure where the competition is fiercer: at the pageant — or at the Baby-sitters Club!

#16 Jessi's Secret Language

Jessi had a hard time fitting in to Stoneybrook. But things got a lot better once she became a member of the Baby-sitters Club! Now Jessi has her biggest challenge yet — baby-sitting for a deaf boy. And in order to communicate with him, Jessi must learn his secret language.

#17 Mary Anne's Bad-Luck Mystery

Mary Anne finds a note in her mailbox. *"Wear this bad-luck charm,"* it says, *"OR ELSE."* Mary Anne's got to do what the note says. But who sent the charm? And why did they send it to Mary Anne? If the Baby-sitters don't solve this mystery soon, their bad luck might never stop!

#18 Stacey's Mistake

Stacey's so excited! She's invited her friends from the Baby-sitters Club down to New York City for a long weekend. But what a mistake! The Baby-sitters are *way* out of place in the big city. Does this mean Stacey can't be the Baby-sitters' friend anymore?

#19 Claudia and the Bad Joke

Claudia's not worried when she hears she has to baby-sit for Betsy, a great practical joker. How much trouble could a little girl cause? *Plenty* . . . and now Claudia might even quit the club. It's time for the Baby-sitters to teach Betsy a lesson. The joke war is on!

#20 Kristy and the Walking Disaster

Kristy's little brother and sister want to play on a softball team, so Kristy starts a ragtag team of her own. With Jackie Rodowsky, the Walking Disaster, playing for them, Kristy's Krushers aren't world champions. But nobody beats them when it comes to team spirit!

#21 Mallory and the Trouble With Twins

Mallory thinks baby-sitting for the Arnold twins will be easy money. They're so adorable! Marilyn and Carolyn may be cute . . . but they're also spoiled brats. It's a baby-sitting nightmare — and Mallory's not giving up!

Dawn's trip to California is better than she could ever imagine. And after one wonderful week, Dawn begins to wonder if she might want to . . . *stay* on the coast with her dad and her brother. Dawn's a California girl at heart — but could she really leave Stoney-brook for good?

WIN A BABY-SITTERS NIGHT SHIRT!

250 Winners!

Introducing...

THE BABY-SITTERS CLUB

G*I*V*E*A*W*A*Y*!

You'll love owning your very own Baby-sitters night shirt! You can win one! All you have to do is enter The Baby-sitters Giveaway. It's easy! Just complete the coupon below and return by May 31, 1989.

Your baby-sitters night shirt is light blue with the official Baby-sitters logo on front! One size fits all!

Rules: Entries must be postmarked by May 31, 1989. Contestants must be between the ages of 7 and 12. The winners will be picked at random from all eligible entries received. No purchase necessary. Valid only in the U.S.A. Employees of Scholastic Inc., affiliates, subsidiaries and their families not eligible. Void where prohibited. The winners will be notified by mail.

Fill in your name, age, and address below or write the information on a 3" x 5" piece of paper and mail to: BABY-SITTERS GIVEAWAY, Scholastic Inc., Dept BSC, 730 Broadway, New York, NY 10003.

Baby-sitters Night Shirt Giveaway

Where did you buy this book?

☐ Bookstore ☐ Drug Store ☐ Supermarket ☐ Other _____
☐ Discount Store ☐ Book Club ☐ Book Fair   specify
_____

Name _____

Birthday _____ Age _____

Street _____

City, State, Zip _____

BSC988